Melody's Blues

Giselle Lumas

ISBN-10: 0981793452
ISBN-13: 978-0981793450

Email the author at: gigilumas@att.net

Visit the author's website at: www.gisellelumas.com

Dedication

To my husband- Michael Lumas, Jr.

Prologue

Melody Roberts wondered what her cousin, Terrence Roberts, could possibly want. He had been immersed in the world of Lisa Johnson for the past few years that Melody wondered if perhaps he'd forgotten family existed. She entered Harold and Belle's, a Creole restaurant in Los Angeles, California. The lighting was dim, but she found her way to a table in a secluded corner. She saw a familiar tall mocha skinned slim yet muscular man with dimples and a dazzling smile sitting alone at a table that was meant for ten. "Mel, hey, I haven't seen you in years. How are you?"

She stuck out her right hand and smiled back at him. As their hands touched, she felt shaky, and an invisible spark caused goose bumps to course throughout her body. "Hi, I know you were Terrence's roommate in college, but I can't remember your name," she admitted.

"Reginald Dempsey but just call me Reggie."

Mel finally managed to remove her hand from his grasp and pointed an index finger at him. "So are you as bad as Terrence says you are?"

He was still grinning, "Probably worse."

She giggled.

"He says you're pretty bad too."

Her mouth went to the side as she contemplated this for a moment. "Well, I have been given an unlimited free pass to be as bad as I want or need to be since I had the worst relationship in history."

He motioned his hand for her to take the seat next to him. She accepted. Terrence's brother Greg appeared with his wife. Two other people Mel had never met before appeared, as well. Soon all ten chairs were filled. Terrence was seated at the head of the table with Lisa to his right. They all ordered and began chatting amongst themselves as they waited for the creole food to arrive.

"You know this is an engagement party, right?" Reggie whispered to Mel.

"What? Terrence doesn't tell me anything anymore. I guess I shouldn't be shocked, though," she said with her voice full of disappointment.

"Yep, he proposed to her last weekend at a restaurant in Westlake Village."

She smirked.

"Reggie, aren't you going to say hello to your soul sister?" A woman with enormous breasts, long dark brown straight hair and a well-rounded behind said. She planted a kiss on his cheek. The woman glanced at Mel and said, "Oh, you're trying to get a new phone number?" She giggled. She turned her attention to Mel and stuck her hand out to shake Mel's, "Hi, I'm Veronica Diaz. Don't worry. I'm not a threat at all. I'm Lisa's best friend. I'm going to be the maid of honor at the wedding." Veronica covered her mouth quickly, "Oh, I wasn't supposed to say anything about the big day yet. Pretend you didn't hear me say anything. But I know Reggie has a bigger mouth than I do and probably already said something, right?"

Mel smiled and nodded. She automatically liked Veronica and hoped to see a lot more of her. "I'm Melody, Terrence's cousin, but you can call me Mel. Yes, Reggie did tell me but are you sure I'm not the maid of honor?"

Veronica quickly snatched her hand away from Mel's grasp and said, "Oh, don't even start with me. I am trying so hard not to swear. I went to confession yesterday, don't make me curse already." She put a hand over her heart and said, "I will jump you here in the restaurant if I have to."

"She really will," Reggie warned Mel.

Mel giggled, waving her hand, "I'm kidding. I didn't even know this was an engagement party before I arrived. Terrence only left a message on my cell phone demanding I meet him and a few others here at six today. We hardly ever talk."

"Really?" Veronica asked, slouching over between her and Reggie. Mel wondered if she did it on purpose for Reggie's benefit because a little more than cleavage was falling out of her low-cut emerald satin or perhaps silk top. "He talks about you all the time. You're more of a sister to him than a cousin."

"Thanks," Mel said.

"So, seriously, did Reggie ask you for your phone number yet? He's not seeing anyone right now. Terrence mentioned you were available too. You two would seriously look cute together, and the babies you will make... ahhh... beautiful. I see you two making at least two babies together. I'd say four, but the economy is atrocious."

Reggie gave Veronica a gentle shove on her shoulder and pointed at the only vacant seat at the table, "I think you need to go... now... really... V."

Mel laughed.

"Oh, I'm saying too much?" Veronica giggled. She put a hand on Mel's shoulder to help her stand up. "Okay, I will be a good girl and go back to my seat. You'll have to give me your phone number Mel before you leave tonight. We will have to coordinate and plan the shower and ladies night."

"Okay, I will."

"You will have to give it to me too," Reggie said as Veronica went back to her seat.

Mel looked at Reggie skeptically. She didn't plan on coming tonight to meet a new prospective boyfriend. She wondered if she should give him a fake number or not. Then again, it seemed as though Veronica would end up giving him the real number.

Nine months later...

Chapter One

"Ow, she's a brick, da dadada... house...." Melody Roberts sang and danced to the music playing from her stereo as she moved around her tiny kitchen. She lifted the lid from the enormous pot of spaghetti sauce that was simmering on her stove. She took a wooden spoon and stirred. The phone rang, and she danced her way to the cordless phone that was on the granite counter top. Glancing at the caller ID she knew it was her cousin's fiancé calling, "Hey Lisa," she said, leaning against a counter, "What's up?" She pressed a button on the remote control to lower the volume.

"Veronica is adamant about having a stripper come over immediately following the bridal shower. I don't want a stripper. She doesn't understand that I only want to see Terrence's naked body. I don't need to see any other man."

Mel rolled her eyes then interrupted Lisa before she could say anything further. "Lisa, you are whining to the wrong person. I agree with Veronica. I want to see a stripper. Stop thinking that the shower and ladies night is about you, okay? The wedding is all about you, but the parties and celebrations before your big day are all about your friends and family." Just then there was a beep on her phone indicating another call had just come through, "Hold on, I have another call."

Before clicking on the other line, she glanced at the caller id again and saw that Veronica was now calling her. She smiled, "Hey V, Lisa is on my other line."

"Mel, she is so uptight! One day she is just going to explode, and it's not going to be pretty. She's driving me loco," Veronica began speaking in Spanish, but Mel couldn't understand what she was saying.

"Why don't I put us all on three-way and we can all talk about this..."

Veronica immediately became louder and sputtered off more Spanish, but this time a lot faster. Finally, Mel heard her take a deep inhale of breath then a slow exhale. "You know what? Just talk to her. Explain that this isn't about her, and she needs to lighten up and stop being so selfish. I'm telling you; I am about to give up being the Maid of Honor and let you handle the stress. She is so controlling! Okay, I need to go meet Pablo for lunch. He's already agreed to strip for free and knows what routine he's going to do. So, like I said, talk some sense into her, or I give up."

Mel giggled, "Pablo is the stripper? The new guy who works for you?"

"Yes, you haven't met him yet so stop laughing... and he doesn't work *for* me, he works **with** me."

"But you said he's gay."

"Look, it's all a fantasy, right?"

Mel's shoulders were shaking with laughter, "You said he gets on your nerves."

"You know what, now you're getting on my nerves too. I have to go. Talk some sense into Miss Control Freak, okay?" Veronica didn't give Mel the chance to answer because she disconnected the call.

Lisa was back on the line, "Let me guess, that was Senorita Super Freak herself. She's calling you to complain about me, and my obsessive compulsive disorder-ish need to control everything and everyone around me, and I need to lighten up and have some fun... oh and shake my cha cha's like I never have before." Lisa spoke almost as fast as Veronica did.

Mel rubbed her temple in circular motions. She wondered if she could have both of their numbers blocked from her phone. But then again, they both knew where she lived and would end up at her condo door repeatedly banging on the door until she finally answered.

"Mel, are you there?" Lisa whined.

"Yes, Lisa, I'm here. She said she was having Pablo strip for free. So what's the problem? You know he's gay, right?"

Mel could hear the gasp of breath coming from Lisa. "What's the point of watching a gay man strip? You know you will never be with him. I just don't get it."

"It's a fantasy, Lisa. Don't you ever use your imagination? Really, you do need to lighten up. Here's what you can do... later down the line when you and Terrence have been together for decades and your sex life hits rock bottom you can one day close your eyes. You can fantasize about Pablo and make love to Terrence with your eyes closed pretending he's Pablo."

Lisa was quiet for a while. Mel put the phone on mute and laughed knowing that Lisa had no idea if she was serious or not.

Finally, Lisa said, "Oh, my gosh! I cannot believe you. You are sick in the head, you know that?"

Mel unmuted her line then said, "And that's why Reggie and I are together. He's just as sick as I am."

"See, you are practically married yourself! Why would you need to see a stripper?"

"Hey, first of all, I'm highly offended," Mel reached for a big pot from one of her lower cabinets and filled it with water and placed it on the stove. She switched the phone to her left ear to give her right shoulder a rest. "You know Reggie, and I don't ever plan on getting married. But, we have been together for over nine months, and I just have the need to see other men's bodies. Seeing a stripper is perfectly healthy. Also, Veronica can tell him only to strip down to a g-string. He doesn't have to be entirely naked."

"Hmmm...." Lisa paused, "okay. Tell her it's okay as long as he keeps his boy toy covered up. I don't want to see it."

Mel grinned, "Okay, I'll tell V."

"One more thing, tell the crazy woman to stop making threats about not being my maid of honor. She knew what she was up against when she agreed. We were roommates all through college... hellooo..."

"Okay, I'll give her the message. I need to focus on my dinner now."

"Fine, I'll see you this weekend."

"Bye," Mel clicked off the phone then focused on the spaghetti. She grabbed a pile of noodles, split them in half with her hands, dumped them in the pot of boiling water then lowered the flame on the stove. Next she put the garlic bread in the oven and tossed the salad. She glanced at the clock on her stove. It was six fifteen. Reggie would be here soon.

She skipped to her master bathroom to freshen up her lipstick and touch up her hair. She kept her brown hair boyish short and curly. She was five two with dark brown

12

eyes and thick eyelashes, mocha skin and a perfect pearly white smile with full lips. Reggie's skin tone was the same as hers, but his hair was jet black, and he was six feet tall. She tended to wear heels whenever they were out. She felt the tingly feeling that she always tended to have whenever she thought of Reggie. She noticed she seemed to have the feeling constantly.

She was wearing a white tank top and tan shorts, bare feet to show off her fresh pedicure with the little flowers painted on each of her big toes. She heard the timer beep in her kitchen then rushed in to check on the noodles and the bread. Both were now ready. A moment later the doorbell rang.

The tingly feeling in her belly intensified, but she skipped to the front door. "Hey baby," she said as soon as she opened the door. Reggie's dimples appeared on both sides of his cheek. He scooped her up into her arms and kissed her hungrily. They both let out a moan.

"Hey," he said in a husky tone, setting her back down to earth and making his way into her condo. "Mmm… it smells real good in here. What are you cooking?"

"Spaghetti. You're right on time. It's ready for us to eat."

She hadn't noticed the bottle of wine he was holding until he placed it on her breakfast bar. "Pinot Grigio will go great then."

Mel only nodded. The wine wasn't something she truly got excited about. She was a simple woman. A cold beer went well with anything in her book. But so did milk. It wasn't as if she liked to drink a lot, only occasionally. She noticed Reggie always seemed to have to have wine whenever they went out to a restaurant and needed to tell her what wines were best with what foods. He tried to have her drink the wine slowly to savor the taste and tried to get her to name the flavors that touched the taste buds. She could only tell him if it was too sweet, not sweet enough, too tarty or too bitter. He seemed to get frustrated with her.

She reached into one of her upper cabinets in her small kitchen and pulled out two plates, handing one to Reggie. "You can go ahead and dish as much as you want." She wondered if Reggie expected her to dish it for him, but he didn't hesitate, he happily accepted the plate from her and immediately began to dish his food. He wandered to the small round glass table that was in front her sliding glass doors leading to her balcony. He reached into his pocket and took out a corkscrew. He uncapped the wine then poured each of them a drink. "This is for you. I figured we should have one here since we know I will be spending a lot of time here." He handed her the brand new corkscrew.

"Okay," Mel answered casually. He didn't seem to notice her lack of enthusiasm over receiving a brand new corkscrew.

She tried not to let it bother her but filed the feelings away for a future conversation or argument. She wondered if she was reading too much into a simple corkscrew. Was she fair to herself by allowing the corkscrew in her home? Could she now be considered as one of the pretentious women who erased any evidence of who she truly was for the sake of keeping a man? Hadn't Reggie known by now (after nine months) that she wasn't a big fan of wine. A part of her realized that he probably didn't because whenever he offered wine to her she accepted it without any comment or complaint. Maybe she needed to let him know the truth now before it went any further. She cleared her throat as she carried her plate to the table and sat across from him. "Reggie, I'm not a big fan of wine, you do know that, right?"

Reggie grabbed his fork and blinked momentarily, "Oh," he cleared his throat then admitted, "No, I didn't. Every time I offered you wine you took it, so I thought you enjoyed it as much as I did."

Mel squinted her nose and shook her head. "Nope, I was just being polite."

"Oh, I'm sorry. I wish you told me sooner. Was it torture going to the Jazz and Wine Festival with me a few weeks ago?"

She took a deep breath, "If it weren't for the music, yes."

His head snapped back a little as if he were just struck in the face. He blinked his eyes for a few moments, cleared his throat then asked, "Okay, so is there anything else I should know?"

She rubbed the back of her neck with her right hand, tilted her head to the side then admitted, "I panic when men try to leave their belongings at my place. One day it's a toothbrush, a hairbrush or comb. Next it's slippers, robes, underwear, and then they try to move in, mess up my credit score and mooch off of me for almost a year."

Reggie dropped his fork and stared at her. "You know I don't want to get that serious, right?"

"Right, this is why I don't want you to start leaving any of your belongings here."

"Um, Mel, the corkscrew was a little gift. It's yours to keep, not mine."

"But I don't drink wine."

Reggie's jaw clenched. "But sometimes your guests do. I'm not just referring to myself. I know Terrence and Lisa both enjoy wine. So think of the corkscrew as a gift for when your family, friends and significant other come to visit."

"Fine," Mel said through clenched teeth. She was not sure why it was still bothering her so much. Was it because he seemed to think he was somehow superior to her because he had the acquired taste for wine? Or was her low self-esteem rising to the surface again? Reggie had graduated from the same college as Veronica, Lisa, and Terrence. She always felt inferior in some ways when she was around them. She lived with Terrence and his family since she was six years old but had moved out on her own when she was eighteen. She was grateful for all that Terrence's family had done for her, but she was an independent free spirit and didn't want to feel she was a burden on anyone. Now she worked for an insurance company and owned her very own condo. It may be small to other people, but it was her pride and joy.

Reggie was studying her. She could tell he had something he wanted to say but didn't say it. They each ate their food in silence. Mel finally broke the silence by asking, "So, as Terrence's best man, what have you planned for the bachelor party?"

He chewed the rest of his bread and said, "Actually, I haven't planned anything yet. Terrence doesn't want the traditional crazy bachelor party."

Mel crossed her arms. "That's a bunch of bull. Why do you feel you need to lie to me? I know my cousin. He used to keep a stack of Playboy magazine's in his closet and had porn tapes stuffed under his bed. He's a freak. I think it runs in our family. The man needs a stripper."

"I...." Reggie frowned.

"Lisa, is getting one. Okay, let me correct myself, V and I are getting one, it honestly doesn't matter if Lisa wants one or not. So, don't try to sit there like a sweet and innocent man when I know you like to play just as much as I do. You can get a stripper. I know you don't need my permission, but I am just clearing the air. Reggie, let's make a deal, here and now. Be honest and straightforward with me and I will show you the same courtesy. I think it is necessary to be honest about who we truly are and not pretend to be someone else because eventually the lies and dishonesty will tear us apart. You cheat on me; I will cheat on you. You hurt me, I hurt you. Karma, plain and simple."

Reggie squinted his eyes then shook his head in disagreement. "Sounds more like wicked payback. It also looks like you don't trust me. Nothing is pure and simple with you Mel."

"What do you mean?"

"Well, take tonight as an example; I was in a great mood. I was ready to enjoy a romantic evening with you. I had been looking forward to it since yesterday when you invited me over. But it just seems like all you want to do tonight is argue. Tonight, you are deliberately picking a fight with me for every little thing."

"What do you mean? Every little thing? It's just a corkscrew and a stripper."

"Okay, maybe I should go…" Reggie stood up. He grabbed his empty plate and walked into the kitchen. He rinsed the plate off then placed it in her dishwasher.

"Maybe you should," Mel said with her arms crossed leaning against her counter top.

"Fine, call me when you are ready to talk like an adult," Reggie said and walked out of her condo, slamming the door behind him.

Mel stared at the door and felt the lump rising in her throat. *What was that about?* Mel wondered. She couldn't even comprehend it herself. She wanted to blame her mixed and weird emotions on someone other than herself. She was apparently trying to pick a fight with Reggie. She just wasn't sure why. Well, that wasn't entirely accurate. Terrence and Lisa's wedding had her thinking too much about the consequences of commitment. She also wondered if she would ever be able to trust anyone ever enough to desire to get married. Mel didn't want to get hurt; plain and simple. She didn't want to lose any of her independence either. She didn't want to be committed to just one person.

The feelings that she had for Reggie were truly scaring her. She wanted to push him away now before she was too deep into the relationship. She knew it didn't make sense, but it didn't matter. She wanted to push him away now. Why put it off any longer? She was used to the people she loved leaving her and never coming back. Look at her mother. She hadn't seen her since the day she dropped her off at Terrence's house.

She didn't want a day without Reggie, but she might as well get used to it. She put the rest of her spaghetti sauce away in the refrigerator and cleaned up the kitchen. Twenty minutes later, she settled in her bedroom with a romance novel. Romance novels always had happy endings. She could count on that but not in her real life.

Chapter Two

The next day Veronica appeared at Mel's doorstep with her enormous purse over her shoulder. Her long brown silky hair was slicked back into a tight ponytail with her signature large silver hoop earrings dangling from each of her ears. She pushed the dark sunglasses on top of her head to look directly into Mel's eyes. "Let's go to the mall. I need to get away. Shopping is the only way."

Mel smiled. "Answer to my prayers. Let me grab my purse and keys."

They drove to the Thousand Oaks Mall with music blasting over Veronica's car speakers. During their shopping escapade, Veronica guided them towards a small booth filled with cell phones near the kids playing area. There was a short overweight man with slightly grayed dark hair pulled back into a ponytail sitting on a stool next to a cash register. His hairline was receding, but he carried himself with confidence. He was tanned, and his face was a little on the shiny, glistening side. Mel considered him to be slightly close to a greasy sleazeball. Mel stopped herself. Who was she to judge someone by appearance? She didn't even know the guy. "Hey V, I thought that was you. Only one I know who looks like Jennifer Lopez."

Veronica grinned widely at that. "Hey Mack, how are you?"

"I'm good. You still need a DJ for the ladies night you were talking about?"

Veronica nodded her head to say yes.

"Well, I think I can do it after all. My sister decided not to come out. What time do you want the music to be ready by?"

Veronica glanced at Mel. Mel asked, "Well, the shower is going to be first, so we don't need the music til later in the evening, right? Will Pablo need a DJ?"

Mack frowned, "Pablo? You cheatin' on me V?"

Veronica crossed her arms, which only accentuated her breasts in a red Victoria Secret form fitting shirt. Mel was envious of Veronica's body. She was still as flat chested as she had been back in junior high school, and here Veronica was the ultimate curvaceous woman with breasts exploding from her shirt. "Mack, you promised you would stop pressuring me... you said..."

Mack got off his stool and moved closer to Veronica. He was even shorter than when he was on the stool. He looked up at Veronica, "Baby... I mean V... I keep my promises." He looked over at Mel and explained, "See, V, doesn't realize she is going to marry me someday. It might take a decade or so, but it's going to happen. I saw it in my dreams. We had beautiful babies and a cute little house. She painted and decorated it the way she wanted to. She has to play with other men right now, but she will come to her senses someday soon."

Mel smiled. She liked Mack. He was cute and sweet in his way. She knew he was serious and yet joking in his way. "I like you, Mack. I wish you luck," Mel said, patting him encouragingly on the shoulder.

"Oh, no, Mel… you did not just encourage him, did you?"

Mel smiled innocently and then shrugged.

Mack tilted his head and asked, "What's your name?"

"Mel."

"That's what I thought she said. Is that seriously your name or is it short for something else?"

"Short for Melody."

"Cute. So do you like music?"

"Yep."

"Great, I'll be sure to play some at the party," he smiled at his joke.

"Mix it up, though," Veronica interrupted, "you know I like Old School, and so does Lisa."

"Okay, but what time do you need me to be there?"

Veronica looked at Mel again.

Mel shrugged her shoulders then reminded Veronica, "It's going to be at your place, and you are the one who talked Pablo into stripping."

"Wait a minute. Is Pablo the name of the stripper? That sounds too much like a friendly name not distant like Fabio or something. Hmm… but then Pablo rhymes with Fabio…" Mack shook his head disapprovingly, "I don't know if I like this…"

Veronica put her hands on her hips, "Then don't DJ."

Mack held his hands up in protest and resignation, "Okay, okay, I'm sorry again. What time is he planning to disrobe?"

This time Mel looked at Veronica. Veronica answered, "I think he will be there around six."

"Okay, so I will get there a little bit before five thirty to set up. Will that give you enough time for the shower?"

"Yep," Veronica and Mel said in unison.

"Okay, and you said it's at your place right V?"

21

"Yep," Veronica said.

"Okay, I'll see you next Saturday." Mack stood on his tippy toes and kissed Veronica on the cheek. He then reached for Mel's right hand and kissed it lightly. "It was a pleasure meeting you, Mel."

Mel smiled, "Nice meeting you too."

"Okay, let's go get something to eat. See you later Mack," Veronica said, tugging on Mel's arm urging her to follow her to the food court. "Why did you do that?"

"Do what?" Mel asked.

"Encourage him to keep bugging me. I told him a thousand times that I only want him as a friend, but he keeps pressuring me to go out on a date with him."

"Oh, V, he seems like a nice guy, why don't you give him a chance?"

"Because... I'm not attracted to him. I don't want to give him any false hopes."

"Well, I don't think you are being fair. I mean the man wishes to marry you..."

"Exactly... I don't see myself with him... can you just not encourage him anymore? He's my friend, and I'd like to keep it that way."

"Fine," Mel said.

They found themselves standing in front of a Chinese food restaurant and decided to go in. Fifteen minutes later, digging into a pile of orange chicken and chow mien Veronica asked Mel, "So how are things with you and Reggie?" Veronica's tone sounded as if she already knew.

"Let me guess you talked to Reggie this morning."

Veronica shook her head side to side as if she were trying to deny it but knew that she couldn't, "Yes, but I want to hear your side."

Mel put down her chopsticks sticks and reached for the fork instead. She was too hungry to try to be coordinated with chopsticks. She jabbed a piece of orange chicken and closed her eyes as she chewed. She let out a moan from satisfaction. Finally, she tilted her head to the side. "I just don't want to get serious."

"Is it that simple?"

"I love Reggie, and I just don't want to get in so deep that either one of us gets hurt."

"Mel, your relationship with Reggie is different from any of the relationships that you have ever had...."

"How would you know? You weren't around when I had my other relationships. You only started hanging out with me when I started dating Reggie..."

"Exactly, I wasn't around. So automatically none of your relationships were the same because you didn't have me around back then," Veronica said holding her chopsticks up in victory.

Mel laughed, "You're crazy V." Mel fiddled with the silver ring that was on her right middle finger. Terrence's mom had given it to her on her eighteenth birthday explaining to her that it was once her great grandmother. According to family history, Mel's great grandmother was an extremely strong and independent woman. Terrence's mom believed Mel was just as strong as her great grandmother.

"But, I speak the truth. You now have my insight and my input. I told you, I minored in Psychology, right?"

"Yes, V," Mel answered, fighting the urge to roll her eyes.

"Now, Reggie is just as scared as you are. You know that he has been dating thousands and thousands of women ever since college, right?"

Mel sighed as if to say yes.

"Okay, but do you know why?"

"Why?" Mel asked in a monotone as she took another orange chicken and chewed.

"Tonya is the reason."

"Who is Tonya?" Mel was suddenly sitting up straighter and listening more attentively to Veronica.

Veronica took a sip of her Sprite then explained, "He and Tonya lived together almost the whole time they were in college. He wanted to marry her, but he found out she had been cheating on him, not just once but a ton of times. He was willing to forgive her, but she broke up with him. She said that he was suffocating her and that she knew he would never truly trust her again. Ever since then he hasn't opened up to anyone. He vowed to have only one night stands until he dies, but apparently you're changing him."

Mel's mouth moved to the side as she thought about this. She hadn't realized that Reggie wanted to marry someone else in the past. The thought had never occurred to her. She just assumed he liked to sleep with many women.

"And you know you are the only woman he has seen for the past nine months? He hasn't been monogamous since Tonya."

Mel felt a lump forming in her throat. Her eyes were beginning to burn.

Veronica touched Mel's hand. "You know me and Reggie are tight, right? We are like this..." Veronica crossed her middle finger around her index finger on her right hand. "He tells me everything. He's my soul brother and always will be."

"Why don't you date him?" Mel sputtered out the question before she could stop herself. It had been an issue that had roamed around her head for months, but she never had the courage to voice it.

Veronica looked at Mel as if all she needed to do was put glasses on to find the answer. Veronica shook her head, "No, no... listen to me, okay? I said he's my soul brother. I can't explain it." Veronica put down her fork and put both of her hands over her heart. "We look out for each other. Did he ever tell you that we were in a bank together when it was robbed? Then about a year later we were at a fast food place at the same time when it was robbed? We had guns to our heads... It's hard to explain what one time having it happen to you but then twice.... And with the same companion... noooo.... Destiny is telling us we would be disastrous if we ever took each other seriously like that. Besides, he's not my type in that way. He doesn't go to church enough either."

Mel's jaw dropped open. Her mind was spinning from so much information that was provided in a matter of seconds. "What? Robbed...no, when..." she held her hands up, "let me guess... back when you were all in college..."

Veronica nodded her head in agreement, "Yes, exactly. Anyway, when that kind of thing happens... you are connected for life."

"Maybe you two shouldn't go to the same places," Mel said frowning.

"Exactly," Veronica said seriously then added, "but listen to me, Mel. Don't hurt Reggie, okay. He will call me every night at the wee hours of the night when I need to get my beauty sleep. He loves you. Give love a chance chica."

Mel cleared her throat then admitted, "I'm scared."

"Why?"

She supposed she could explain how everyone leaves her eventually, but she just didn't want to. She didn't like feeling sorry for herself and she especially didn't like crying in front of others. "I don't know. I just am."

"Well knock it off. Call Reggie and talk to him. Okay?"

"Fine, I'll call him tonight."

"Thank you, you will feel better. Trust me."

Just then Veronica's pink covered cell phone rang, "Hola, coma esta?" She continued speaking in Spanish and ignoring Mel sitting at the table. Veronica giggled several times, gasped a few times and then sputtered off more Spanish.

Mel was full from eating by the time Veronica finally clicked off her cell phone and dropped it back into her enormous purse. "That was Pablo. He wants to go out tonight."

"You two seem to be seeing a lot of each other."

Veronica beamed and appeared to glow. "Yep, he's so much fun, and he makes me laugh. He's like a sister I never had."

Mel tilted her head to the side then said, "Wait, I thought you have two sisters in Florida."

Veronica frowned, "Yes, exactly, he's like the sister I never had. My real sisters are mean, self-absorbed, materialist, conniving and did I say mean, awful, mean... Oh... you have no idea." She took a sip of her soda and reached for the bill that the waitress had just placed at their table. "It's my treat since I was rudely talking on the phone most of the time." Veronica handed the waitress her charge card before Mel could stop her.

Neither one of them had bought anything from their shopping adventure. They only window shopped and tried on clothes for the fun of it. Veronica drove Mel home then said, "You promised... call Reggie tonight, okay?"

"Fine," Mel said as she stepped out of Veronica's car.

When Mel unlocked the door to her condo, she felt immediately lonely. Veronica had temporarily filled a void in her day, but there was still the void in her heart. Veronica was right, she needed to call Reggie and set things straight. She dropped her purse on the oak coffee table and wandered into her bedroom looking for her cordless phone. She slipped her shoes off then lay on her bed with the phone in her hand. She counted to ten then dialed Reggie's number.

Reggie answered on the third ring. "Hi Mel," he sounded insecure.

"Hey," they were both quiet for a few long seconds. Finally, Mel admitted, "I don't know why I wanted to fight. I don't know why I am trying to push you away… Okay… that's a lie. I know that I am pushing you away for my pride's sake. I keep thinking that one day you are going to realize that you certainly don't want to be with me, and you will eventually leave. So I want to save myself some heartache by pushing you out of my life now before we get any deeper."

"That's what I thought," Reggie said in his I-know-all tone of voice that was bothering her lately.

"You know what? That's another thing. And I'm not trying to start a fight now… but there has been this little nagging inside my head about you. I couldn't quite put my finger on, and I just realized what it is."

"What?" Reggie asked, sounding innocent.

"You act as though you are superior to me. I mean take the wine for example. You seemed to be so disappointed in me. You acted as if I failed some test when I told you that I honestly am not that crazy about wine. You always act as if you know everything or that you know more than I do. It's like just because you went to college, and I didn't that you are somehow better or greater than I am. I think you need to stop acting as if you know everything because, guess what?"

"What?" Reggie asked innocently again.

"You don't know everything. You don't know me very well, even though we've gone out for nine months, and you don't know everything about the universe... at least not *my* universe."

She heard him sigh a small sigh; finally he said, "Mel, I know I don't know everything. I know I have a lot to learn about you. I want to get to know the real you. We both are new to the relationship zone, so I don't..."

"See.... That right there is incorrect. I am not new to the relationship zone. I lived with someone for a year, and he cheated on me repeatedly and messed up my credit. It took him running off to Vegas to marry the mother of his baby to get him out of my place. So don't think that I am new to relationships. I've been lied to. Don't think that I don't have experience in the love department..."

Reggie interrupted her, "Well, for me this is new or almost new. Mel, I haven't been in a one woman relationship in an exceedingly long time. So if, I say anything or do anything to offend you or hurt you, you have to let me know right away. I want us to be true to each other too. You aren't the only one who is scared."

"I didn't say I was scared!" Mel yelled.

"You don't have to..."

"Oh, let me guess... you just know... because you know everything."

"Why are you trying to turn this into an argument again? Mel, I'm trying...."

Mel interrupted him again, "Reggie, I am not attempting to argue. I am discussing my feelings. *We* are debating our emotions."

"Mel, you try to be this fierce independent woman when you aren't that tough. Why don't you stop feeling so insecure and allow me to love you the way you genuinely deserve? Stop fighting me."

Mel wasn't sure what to say. He verbally hit her in the gut.

"I was hoping we could go out tonight, but I think we both still need a little space. Try calling me again when you are ready to go out," Reggie said and disconnected the call before she could get another word out.

Mel plopped back down to a laying position on her bed and stared up at her ceiling. *What just happened?* She was supposed to be the one in control of the phone conversation. How had it been twisted and turned around? How had she lost sight of her goal? She meant to apologize for starting the argument yesterday but ended up starting a whole new one. Maybe she was still defining what her argument was. *Yes, that's it. I need to figure out what we are arguing about.* Mel thought.

Chapter Three

The next day Mel woke to hear the radio alarm go off, and immediately she felt the Monday blues. She took her shower, ate a bagel and carried her container of coffee with her to her car. The drive to the health insurance company where she worked was pleasant, not too much traffic. She sauntered into the building not looking forward to taking customer service phone calls from unhappy insured members. Lisa had evidently been at her desk because there was a bright green sticky stuck to her monitor saying, "Meet me in the caf at 12:30 for lunch. Lisa."

Mel groaned. She didn't like meeting Lisa for lunch while they were working. When Mel took lunch, she liked to be far away from work as possible and avoid as much stress as possible. Lisa didn't know how to relax and just eat lunch. She would predictably talk non-stop about the wedding and manage to squeeze in some work related topic into her monolog, as well. Mel loved and respected Lisa. She was genuinely happy that Lisa knew how to make her anal retentive cousin Terrence happy too. But... Can't she just say no? *Of course not,* Mel answered herself. Besides she was appreciative to Lisa for assisting her with landing the job. Lisa was a manager of one of claims customer service departments and had personally recommended Mel.

By lunch time, Mel had answered over fifty customer service calls and was ready to run out of the building. She groaned, opened her desk drawer and pulled out her wallet from her purse.

The cafeteria wasn't too crowded. She found the tall light skinned woman with long chemically straightened auburn hair standing in line, waiting for chicken strips and French fries. "Thank you for meeting me, Mel," Lisa said, her hazel cat like eyes met Mel's.

"No problem," Mel lied. She examined the menu and decided on a bean burrito with guacamole and sour cream.

Moments later they walked with lunch trays in their hand to the patio and sat at one of the circular tables with a forest green umbrella for shade. "So what's going on?"

"I'm not sure I want to marry Terrence," Lisa confessed right after sitting down in one of the green plastic chairs.

Mel popped open her soda and groaned, "You're just scared Lisa. You know he loves you."

Lisa shook her head in disagreement, "No, it's more than just wedding jitters. He honestly gets on my last nerve. I was trying to explain that to Veronica the other day, but she was so caught up in the bridal shower and ladies night she wouldn't hear anything that I had to say."

"Well, maybe you really shouldn't be talking to me or Veronica about this. You should be talking to Terrence."

Lisa let out an aggravated sigh, "I need to talk to someone else first before I confront him..."

"Well... what has Terrence been doing that's been driving you so crazy?"

"He suffocates me. I can't go to the bathroom without him wondering what I'm doing. I scratch my nose, and he asks me if my nose itches…. It's like hellooooo… What do you think? I just feel like I can't have a single thought or do one little thing on my own. He has to be involved in everything that I do."

"That's just because he loves you so much Lisa. Don't call off the wedding just talk to him. You will crush him if you call off the wedding."

Lisa put her elbows on the table and dropped her forehead into her hands. Her voice sounded muffled, but Mel could still hear her when she said, "The other day, I washed towels, and he took them out of the dryer." Lisa announced as though the experience crushed her.

Mel frowned not sure what the big deal was about towels and someone else taking them out of the dryer. Personally, she would be happy if Reggie did any part of her laundry duty.

Lisa let her hands drop and looked at Mel then explained, "I have this thing about towels ever since I was a kid. I have to be the one to take them out of the dryer right after the dryer stops. I love the way they feel against my skin, nice, warm and fluffy…" Lisa smiled at the confession.

"Wow," Mel managed to mumble.

"I know it sounds stupid, but that was just one thing. What upset me was Terrence asked me where he should put the towels after he folded all of the towels… and folded them wrong I might add…. Can you see where I'm getting at?"

"Um… it's sounds like obsessive compulsive disorder to me," Mel mumbled, not sure if Lisa heard her. Mel's lips became small, and she nodded in agreement. "Okay… so

Terrence has been living with you for a while, and he still doesn't know where he should put the towels."

Lisa let out a sigh of relief then said, "Thank you. Finally, someone understands."

"You have a severe case of pre-wedding jitters," Mel said then finally took a bite of her burrito. She could see Lisa staring at her from the corner of her eye. Before making direct eye contact with her, she took a sip of her soda. "I understand Lisa. He's interfering with your routine. He's crowding you and interrupting your thoughts, but that's no real reason to call off the wedding. You are connected to Terrence. It's too late for you to back away from him now. You have to talk to him. Which seems to be the theme lately for me and Reggie.... talking... communication. Sure it might turn into an argument, but you have to be honest with him. He isn't a mind reader, you know? How is he going to ever know you have a thing about the towels if you never told him? How is he going to know he's suffocating you if you never tell him?"

"But don't you see? He asked me where he should put the towels," Lisa waved her arms around animatedly and with a pained expression on her face. "He's lived with me for four months, and he still doesn't know where the towels go? Does he expect me to wait on him or does he seriously not want to live with me? He should know where everything in the house goes by now, you know? I mean, maybe it's all a gigantic neon sign that is saying that he genuinely doesn't want to get married either."

"I think you are just scared, which seems to be my problem too." Mel took another bite of her burrito.

Lisa had barely touched her lunch but took a sip of her orange juice. They sat quietly together for a while finally Lisa said, "Maybe your right. I'm used to living on my own, you know?"

"Yep, you're used to doing whatever you want to do and when you want to do it. You aren't used to having to please someone else or think of someone else's feelings or opinion. You aren't going to be able to just buy whatever you want, at least not the big purchases. You will always have to consult him. Never mind about the I-AM-THE-MAN syndrome. Everyman has to feel like he is the man, never mind that the woman works just as hard as he does..." Mel was getting irritated.

Lisa held her hands up in resignation, "Okay, I get it. Yes, you're right. I'll talk to him tonight."

Mel finished her lunch before Lisa and leaned back in her chair and briefly closed her eyes. When she opened her eyes, she saw that Lisa had finally finished her lunch and was now staring at her.

"So you and Reggie are having problems?"

Mel took a deep intake of breath then let it out slowly. "We aren't on the same wavelength."

"He said you think he thinks he's superior to you."

"Does he tell everyone about every argument we have? Yesterday, Veronica talked to me about him and now you. Does he know how to keep our personal business to himself?" Now, Mel was officially cranky. She was perfectly fine before meeting Lisa, which was one of the reasons she didn't want to meet her.

"He doesn't think he's superior to anyone. Reggie is one of the most giving people I know. He just wants to make you happy."

"Will you knock it off? I didn't ask for your opinion, okay? You asked me to meet you today to talk about your issues. You can stay out of mine, all right?" Mel rose from the chair and dumped her trash. "I have to get back on the phone. I'll talk to you later."

Lisa didn't say anything as Mel walked away.

Mel hadn't heard from Reggie until Wednesday night when he unexpectedly appeared on her doorstep step with flowers and sad eyes. She had just finished doing the dishes and had a dishrag in her hand when she opened the door. "I'm sorry," Reggie said.

Mel crossed her arms. "For what? I thought I was the one in the wrong."

"I'm sorry for talking about our personal problems with other people. I'm sorry for making you feel inferior. I just want to love you, Mel."

She felt the little wall she had built around her heart crumble a little. She reached for the flowers then he reached for her and embraced her in a hug. "You feel magnificent."

"You too," she said as she pulled him into her condo.

They lay on her bed an hour later. Mel was resting her head on Reggie's chest listening to his heartbeat. His left arm was wrapped around her while his right was curled up on his head. "I don't know what to do for Terrence's bachelor party. I mean, sure if it were a year ago, I would have taken him to Vegas or something but now... I don't know. Plus I'm scared of Lisa."

Mel giggled. "Don't get stressed over it. It isn't that big of a deal."

"But it is, though. Terrence is my best friend. We've been through a lot together. I want his last day as a single man to be special, but I don't know what to do. Do I do the cliché and throw him the wild party everyone is expecting me to? Do I do something altogether different? A poker party or... or... I don't know."

"Why not throw him the wild party everyone is expecting, why disappoint? Hold up to your reputation."

Reggie shook his head in disagreement. "No, I'm just not that person I used to be. I don't think I ever wanted to be the wild man I was."

Mel lifted her head and looked at him with surprise. "Really?"

"Really," he said sincerely, "I was missing something for a long time. I didn't realize what it was until I started dating you Mel."

Mel felt overwhelmed, "No one ever said that to me before."

"I love you, Mel."

She gasped, and her heart skipped a beat. "I love you too Reggie," she finally confessed.

They kissed.

Reggie stayed the night. He admitted to having a duffle bag of clothes in his trunk he'd brought with him just in case. Mel made each of them an omelet, toast and coffee the following morning. "You really can cook Mel. Why are you working as a customer service rep, you should be a chef or own your restaurant."

Mel grinned at that and planted a kiss on his lips. "I use to pretend to be a chef when I baked or cooked in my Aunt Jane's kitchen. Thank you."

"I'm not just saying it. You should think about it. You seem so happy when you're cooking too."

She nodded. She had always had secret dreams of becoming a world class chef and owning tons of restaurants throughout the world. "Well, maybe one decade I'll go to culinary school." She glanced at the clock on her stove then said, "Right now I think both of us need to leave to go to work."

Reggie groaned, "Can't we call in sick?"

"I'd love to, but there are too many people out on leave in my department right now. I really can't skip out on my team."

Reggie got up and stretched. He gave Mel another hug. Mel didn't want him to let go. It felt so good to be in his arms. She felt safe and protected.

Chapter Four

Saturday afternoon Mel drove to Veronica's house early to help decorate for Lisa's bridal shower. It was to take place out on Veronica's patio. They decorated using pink, magenta and white streamers along with white paper bells. The Santa Ana winds were starting to blow, but it wasn't too bad. Mel only had to redo the streamers once. It was a warm day in Simi Valley, California with clear blue skies. Mel started sneezing. Veronica gave her an allergy pill that helped but began to make her a little drowsy by the time the bridal shower started. They played a few games, ate cake and then Lisa finally started opening the gifts. There were a few naughty gag gifts from Mel and Veronica, which Lisa was too embarrassed to show to the other thirty ladies that attended the party.

Although Lisa's skin was normally a caramel complexion, her face turned bright red each time she came across a gag gift. The majority of the remaining gifts were lingerie.

Finally, around four o'clock several women had started to leave. By the time Mack arrived, only fifteen women had remained. Mel hadn't noticed a short blond woman until Lisa began to talk to her. She reminded her of

Tinker Bell. Her hair was short and spiky in the back. She was thin but muscular. Something about her made Mel want to eavesdrop on their conversation. She sat close by in one of the folding chairs so she could listen.

"Yes, it's been awhile since I last saw you. So what have you been up to?" Lisa asked her.

"I moved to Phoenix, Arizona for a few years. I was a producer at a radio station and was offered a phenomenal job here in LA. I still can't believe you are marrying Terrence. I remember you two were always arguing with each other in college. It seemed as though you two couldn't stand one another."

Lisa smiled and nodded in agreement, "Yep, it's sometimes a shock to me too. I guess we were both trying to fight off the strong attraction we felt for each other. We wanted to meet our own educational and career goals first before we were involved in a serious relationship. But, it all worked out."

The woman smiled, "Yep, it did."

"So Tonya, do you think you are here to stay?" Lisa asked.

Tonya? Hmmm... Mel wondered if it was the same Tonya Reggie had been engaged to. She suddenly felt uneasiness in her stomach. Tonya was beautiful. Unfortunately, Mel couldn't hear the rest of Lisa and Tonya's conversation because Mack asked loudly, "So, V, you wanna go out with me next weekend?" He was almost done connecting his laptop to enormous speakers on the patio. Conversation on the patio seemed to come to a halt to hear Veronica's reply.

Veronica walked up to Mack and stood rather close mumbling something that only he could hear. He smiled and nodded his head. "Okay, I'm sorry," Mack said.

Mel wondered what Veronica said to Mack that made him apologize, but before she could ask the doorbell rang. Veronica went go answer it. A tall, muscular man with tanned skin and long silky dark hair entered the patio. Veronica introduced him to everyone, "Ladies, this is Pablo. He's a friend of mine and has agreed to share his body with all of us, but I have to remind you, he's for eyes only. No touching unless you want to tip him, but even that has limits, okay?"

All of the women cheered. Veronica whispered something in Pablo's ear then pointed at Lisa. He nodded with a smile then handed Mack a CD. Currently, Pablo was wearing white linen top and pants with sandals. Prince's *Until the End of Time* began playing over the stereo. It was one of Lisa's favorite songs. Lisa looked nervous and uneasy. Pablo started to dance and removed the rubber band from his hair allowing his dark wavy hair to fall over his shoulders. He made his way towards Lisa, who started to squirm increasingly the closer he came to her. He slowly started unbuttoning his shirt, and the women started screaming again. A few women began tucking money down his underpants. He led Lisa to one of the folding chairs and made her sit in the center of all the women and gave her his version of a lap dance.

Mel's throat was dry. She went to stand right next to Veronica, who was watching Pablo from a distance, "Dang, are you sure he's gay? Look at his back. It's soo..."

"Mmmm... defined. He's into Pilates and cares about the environment. He's a computer wizard."

They both stared at him as he performed. Mel was transfixed although she had a lingering guilt in the back of her mind and longing for Reggie. She frowned. In the past, her relationships never crossed her mind during ladies night. Why would thoughts of Reggie enter her mind now?

It was only ladies night. Why should she suddenly feel guilty?

Finally, Pablo was down to his g-string when the time the music stopped. He planted a gentle kiss on Lisa's cheek and said, "Congratulations, I wish you a lifetime of happiness in your marriage."

He held his right hand out and helped Lisa rise. She appeared to be shaky. "To the Bride!" Pablo shouted in a slight Spanish accent then bowed.

Everyone cheered.

Tonya complained, "That's it? What a rip?"

Veronica immediately approached Tonya and explained, "He's a friend Tonya. Let it go. He did this as a favor to me. Lisa didn't even want a stripper."

Tonya was quiet after that.

Mack began playing dance music, and the ladies started dancing on the patio as Veronica began making margaritas in her kitchen. Mel passed the drinks around. Time was slipping away. Mack had a few of his guy friends show up. Mel was having a good time, but around nine o'clock the doorbell rang again. When Veronica answered the door, she started arguing with someone and attempted to close the door on them but whoever was on the other side of the door was apparently stronger than her. Mel went to see what all the commotion was about.

"Reggie, no... this is for ladies only," Veronica insisted still pushing on the door trying to close it on him.

"What's going on?" Mel asked standing a few feet away from Veronica.

Both Reggie and Veronica paused for a moment to look at Mel. Reggie took advantage of the distraction and was able to finally pry the door all the way open. Seven men followed Reggie; among them was the groom,

Terrence. "We all voted and decided to have the Bachelor party here with you ladies," the men laughed.

Veronica cursed in Spanish but couldn't stop them from entering her home and making their way to her patio. Mel couldn't stop them either. Before Mel could even reach out to give Reggie a hug he was already outside on the patio with Terrence and the other men. She heard Tonya screech, "Reggie!" The next the thing she knew, Tonya had her arms and legs wrapped around Reggie in a tight grasp. Reggie was holding her up with his hands visibly on her tight buttocks. Mel's blood raced throughout her body. Her eyes and throat burned. Her jaw clenched. Mel grabbed her purse and keys and rushed out of Veronica's place without saying goodbye to anyone.

By nine-thirty Mel was in her pajamas and curled in a ball in her bed. She had been crying ever since she came home. Her eyes felt puffy, and her lips felt swollen. She tried to remove the image of Reggie holding Tonya out of her mind, but the memory was a permanent fixture burned into her brain. Mel was angry with herself for crying but hurt too much to stop the tears from falling.

Reggie had called her repeatedly leaving voicemail messages on both her land line and on her cell phone. Mel turned the ringer off on both phones and turned the volume all the way down on her answering machine. No words would be able to erase what her eyes saw for themselves. She knew what she knew, and that was the end of it. Reggie had been overjoyed to allow Tonya back into his life. He hadn't even bothered to acknowledge Mel even when he had made eye contact with her at the front door.

Mel successfully managed to avoid everyone until the following Saturday, which was the day of Lisa and Terrence's wedding. Mel was one of the bride's maids while Reggie was the best man. She supposed there would be no way she would be able to avoid him today, but she was determined to try. They were getting dressed at Veronica's house when Veronica asked in an attempt to clarify, "You know Tonya doesn't mean anything to him, right?"

Mel shook her head in disagreement, "V, don't even bring him up right now. I just want to make it through the wedding then go home to bed."

Veronica looked at her with disappointment in her eyes. "I'm sorry I even invited her. I don't know why I did. I ran into her at the mall, and my mouth just invited her without consulting my brain. I'm sorry chica. I feel like it's my fault." Veronica gave Mel a hug.

"It's okay. I needed to see what I saw. Now I know how he feels."

Veronica shook her head of beautiful shiny hair in disagreement but didn't say anything further.

Lisa appeared in her wedding dress carrying a veil. "Help me," she said frantically looking at them both. "I can't get this thing on with my hair plastered to my head like concrete."

Veronica grabbed the veil while Mel grabbed bobby pins. Lisa sat in a chair in front of Veronica's bedroom mirror while the two of them worked at strategically securing the veil atop her head.

Lisa surprisingly seemed to relax after the veil was in place. They had a few extra minutes before a limo would arrive to pick them up. Mel didn't understand how Lisa and Terrence would agree to waste money on renting a limo when she or Veronica could have easily driven her the few miles to the church. She felt herself getting cranky. She knew she was being selfish but a wedding was the last place she wanted to be right now. Veronica whispered to

Mel, "Snap out of it at least for a little while for your cousin and Lisa's sake, okay? I will tell Reggie to leave you alone."

Mel nodded in agreement and tried to put a smile on. She admitted smiling did seem to lift her spirits up a bit... a tiny microscopic bit.

The wedding ceremony went by in a blur for Mel. She was successful in not making eye contact with Reggie. After the ceremony, photographs were repeatedly taken. She managed to plaster a smile on her face through the entire ordeal. Then off to the reception they went. It was located at a community recreation room. Food had been catered, round tables covered with white and magenta table cloths, expensive flowers on each table along with a bottle of Champaign, disposable camera, and balloons. Chatter filled the room when Mel was announced to enter the room. Finally, the bride and groom entered, and everyone cheered. Mel frowned again at the expensive decorations and food. She was all for celebrating a special occasion but the money involved was ridiculous for one day. She thought it was probably just her crabbiness, and she needed to shake it off.

Reggie somehow managed to stand right next to her during the bride and groom's first dance. "I'm sorry Mel. Are you ever going to talk to me again?"

"Why don't you just leave me alone? You did an excellent job of it last weekend at the party," Mel said and walked away to talk to Terrence's older brother Greg.

"Hey cuz," Mel said to Greg, who was a heftier and bald version of Terrence with caramel skin and light brown eyes.

Greg smiled and scooped her up in a teddy bear hug, her feet dangling more than a foot off the ground. "Hey

Mel, how are you? You look a little blue munchkins." She couldn't help but smile. Greg had called her munchkins since she was little.

"Man problems," she answered honestly knowing she'd never be able to lie to Greg.

"Uh oh. You want me to beat him up for you. You know as a cop I can cover the whole thing up, and no one would ever know."

Mel giggled.

"See that, you just lit the whole place up with your big beautiful smile. That's the Mel I know."

She was still smiling.

"So tell me about. Talking about it helps."

Mel explained everything to Greg in a few short minutes. He nodded in agreement, "Well, Reggie had better open up his eyes and realize the gift before him. I remember him dating Tinker Bell. If I recall right, she was hitting on me when they were engaged one time. I don't think you have too much to worry about."

"You sure?" Mel asked full of doubt.

"I know you, Mel. You are strong, smart, compassionate and beautiful inside and out. Reggie isn't stupid. He just needs to figure out a way to show you he loves you. Now, why don't we stop talking and start dancing? Hey, let's get the electric slide going…" he grinned and grabbed her hand pulling her out onto the dance floor before she could refuse. They danced almost non-stop. Mel didn't notice Reggie watching her from a distance the whole night.

Chapter Five

Wednesday the following week Mel had just got off of work and tossed her keys and purse on her glass table when her cell phone vibrated. She saw that it was Veronica calling, "Hey Mel, wanna meet me for dinner? We can go to the new Mexican restaurant in Chatsworth. I'll drive."

"Okay, but this time it's my treat."

Veronica let out a sigh but agreed, "Fine. I'll pick you up in thirty minutes, okay."

"Okay," Mel said before disconnecting then took a quick shower to freshen up a bit.

"I am so glad the wedding is finally over; you have no idea the amount of stress and pressure I was under. There were a couple of times I considered asking one of my cousins to jump Lisa for me," Veronica admitted an hour later when they were seated at a quiet table.

Mel giggled as she dipped a corn chip into the freshly made salsa.

"Pablo is going to meet us here. I hope you don't mind."

Mel waved her hand nonchalantly, "As long as you didn't invite Reggie or Tonya I'm cool with it." She took a sip of her blended margarita.

Pablo appeared at the table in jeans and a plain white t-shirt. His muscles bulged from under the shirt. A woman would have to be insane to not want to rip the shirt off of him. Both Mel and Veronica sighed from the sight of him.

"Hola ladies," Pablo greeted.

"Hey baby," Veronica said as she scooted over in the booth and patted the seat next to her. "Have a seat."

"Thanks," Pablo said as he sat down then kissed Veronica on the cheek.

Mel stuck her right hand out and said, "Hi Pablo, I'm Mel. I saw you briefly at the shower a couple weeks ago."

"Oh, yeah, nice to see you again. You didn't stay very long after the guys showed up."

"That's a sore subject with her right now. Don't mention it," Veronica told him.

"Por que?" Pablo asked.

"Did you notice the woman who resembles Tinker Bell jumping on the guy who first barged in?" Mel asked Pablo.

He nodded his head to say yes.

"Well, the man who barged in was supposed to be my boyfriend and Tinker Bell is his ex-fiancé. Now you see why I left so suddenly?"

Pablo's thick eyebrows rose, "Oy, I'd say that's a lot of drama."

Veronica gave him a light shove on his shoulder, but Mel laughed. She rose her margarita glass and said, "I'll drink to that," then took a sip.

Pablo took a sip of Veronica's blended margarita when the waitress reappeared he ordered himself one as well but on the rocks instead. They each placed their order as well.

Mel noticed Pablo was sitting closer to Veronica than necessary. There was plenty of room in the booth, but yet their bodies were touching. He reached for Veronica's hand and held it for a few moments. Veronica didn't pull it away.

Mel was tempted to ask Pablo if he truly was gay but thought Veronica wouldn't appreciate it. "So how did you meet your boyfriend?" Pablo asked.

"Pablo stop being so nosy."

"It's okay," Mel said, "He's my cousin's best friend. The groom, Terrence is my cousin. They were roommates in college. I've known Reggie for a long time and always thought he was attractive but never thought of dating him. But when Terrence and Lisa had announced their engagement Reggie, and I were both there at the party, and we were both free..." Mel felt herself smiling at the memory, "He invited me to a reggae club afterwards, and we saw each other every weekend since then... well, almost every weekend."

Veronica wrapped an arm around Pablo and tilted her head on his shoulder. "Hey, do you want to go to the movies after this?" Veronica asked. Mel knew she was deliberately changing the subject.

"I have to go to work for a couple of hours, but you two go ahead."

Veronica frowned, "Why do you have to go to work? There aren't any special projects or anything?"

"I just have a couple of things to go over with Sam."

"The president of the company Sam?" Veronica asked suspiciously.

"Yes," Pablo said too quickly. Mel noticed Veronica seemed irritable. Pablo, on the other hand, appeared suddenly nervous. *Hmmm... Maybe he is having an affair with Sam... or something... hmmmm.... Something isn't right here.* Mel kept her thoughts to herself, but she knew Veronica was thinking the same.

Veronica sat up and scooted over about an inch away from Pablo and began eating the chips and salsa.

The waitress reappeared with their orders. Mel had a simple platter of taquitos with rice and beans. Pablo and Veronica had each ordered a tamale and enchilada with rice and beans. They were quiet as they ate. Mel bit into her guacamole and sour cream covered taquito. She moaned from the delicious crispy taste and closed her eyes as she chewed. *Reggie would like this restaurant.* Visions of his dimples and a perfect smile came to mind. She felt her stomach flutter. Instead of squashing the feeling she reveled in it for a moment. Maybe she could love him from a distance. It was safer that way.

She opened her eyes to see Veronica and Pablo staring at her. She nearly jumped from the unexpected intensity of Veronica's stare. "What?" Mel asked.

"You were completely in your own Reggie world just now, weren't you? Moaning and closing your eyes. Chica, you've got it bad."

Pablo nodded in agreement but didn't say anything. He kept eating.

Mel rolled her eyes and denied, "The taquitos are sooo good. You want to try one?"

"No, I can make them. Psst... I can make all of this at the table," Veronica said with a flourish. "Ah, you should try my menudo someday."

Both Pablo and Mel looked at her doubtfully, "V, you can't even make mac and cheese from the box. What are you talking about?" Pablo asked. Mel tried to stifle a giggle but wasn't successful.

Again Veronica playfully shoved Pablo, "You've never tried my Mexican food." She raised an index finger at Mel in warning, "And neither have you! So both of you... be quiet."

Mel seriously doubted Veronica's cooking abilities but let it go.

Twenty minutes later Pablo glanced at his watch then announced, "I have to go meet Sam now. I'll call you tonight?" Pablo asked Veronica.

Veronica smirked but said, "Sure."

Pablo kissed Veronica on the cheek before scooting out of the booth then gave Mel a pat on the shoulder. "Nice to have lunch with you, Mel. I hope you and Reggie work things out."

"Pablo....?" Veronica whined his name in a tone of a question.

"I'm honest. I'm actually meeting Sam. Trust me V. I'll call you later."

Mel silently watched Pablo as he walked away then handed a black credit card to the waitress whispering something in her ear. Less than a minute later the waitress reappeared with his card and receipt. Pablo put the card back in his pocket and signed. He waved again to Mel and Veronica then disappeared out the door. The waitress came to their table and announced, "He paid for your lunch and said you can order dessert if you like."

Mel grinned and ordered fried ice cream, but Veronica frowned and refused to order anything further.

"What is he up to?" Veronica said under her breath.

"I was wondering the same thing V. I don't think he's gay. He's probably pretending. He's obviously into you."

Veronica shook her head vigorously in denial. "That's not what I'm talking about. Why would a new employee need to meet with the president of the company? I've been with the company for ten years, and I haven't even met with the president and I'm supposedly one of the top employees. I'm the one clients ask for personally to come out and fix their computers. Why is he meeting Sam? That's not fair."

Mel's eyebrows rose. "Wow, you're jealous of Pablo?"

Veronica shook her head vigorously again. "No, I'm angry, not jealous. What kind of crap are they pulling?"

"Maybe you should ask?"

"I tried," Veronica said crankily. "You were sitting right here. You saw me. He looked nervous too. Hmmm... He's keeping something from me."

Mack suddenly scooted into the seat next to Veronica. Mel's eyes widened. Where on earth had he come from?

"What the..." Veronica began.

"I was delivering cell phones to a company across the street and saw your car," Mack explained casually.

Mel narrowed her eyes suspiciously at Mack. She wondered if Mack somehow followed them here and waited for Pablo to leave.

"I only came over to say hi."

Veronica seemed to tense up a bit but said, "Hi Mack." She even managed to put on a smile.

"So what are you two up to today?" He asked.

"Just got off work and got hungry," Mel answered. "What are you up to?"

"I have to run back to the mall and work until closing. As I said, I just had to make a delivery. Hey, would you want to go to a club this weekend V?"

"Maybe..." Veronica sighed then said, "I don't know."

"What's the matter?" Mack asked sincerely.

Veronica shook her head then shrugged her shoulders. "I don't know. Believe it or not I'm getting tired of the clubs."

"What?" Mack and Mel said disbelieving in unison.

"Yeah, I want to stay home this weekend. Sorry, Mack."

Mack leaned into Veronica. She scooted over, but he scooted over too. "Well, I can rent some movies and bring some fried chicken or something."

"Maybe, I'll think about it and call you on Friday. Is that okay?"

"Sure," Mack said. He planted a kiss on Veronica's cheek, stood up then leaned over to give Mel a kiss on the cheek too. "I'll see you later ladies."

He walked away.

The waitress finally arrived with Mel's order of fried ice cream. When she took a bite, she moaned and closed her eyes again as she chewed. There were bits of coconut in the shell. She hadn't had ice cream in a while, so the vanilla ice cream felt ravenous on her tongue.

"Mel, the way you eat must drive men crazy. You look and sound like you're having an orgasm."

Mel opened her eyes wide and said, "Oh, don't even mention sex, I haven't had an orgasm in two weeks how am I supposed to function, you know what I mean?"

Veronica shook her head, "No, I don't know what you mean."

Mel smirked, "Of course you look like a super model you must have it on a regular basis."

"Yes, I have an orgasm on a regular basis but it isn't by the way you think," Veronica said annoyed.

"Huh?" Mel said not able to take another bite of her ice cream.

"I'm still a virgin," Veronica said proudly.

Mel's jaw dropped.

"Not that it's any of your business, but everyone always makes rude assumptions about me. Just because I have a sexy style doesn't mean I put out. I am a devout

Catholic. I am not going to give my innocence away to anyone but my husband."

Mel was shocked but then asked, "Wait, then what was up with the stripper if you're so innocent?"

"I look but don't touch. I kiss, I hug, but I don't let anyone touch my hooey."

Mel giggled. "Well, I'm impressed. Good for you."

Veronica fanned herself, "Pablo though is going to kill me."

Mel laughed.

"The man has a body that will make me sin. I have to be strong, though."

"Well, pray for me because I am so not a virgin."

"Yeah, I have been praying for you and Reggie. I will keep praying. Hey, want to go to church with me on Sunday?" Veronica asked nonchalantly.

"Sure, maybe a miracle will happen," Mel said. She finished her ice cream then the two of them walked out of the restaurant. It was dark outside. Mel glanced at the time on her cell phone. "We've been in there for almost two and half hours."

"Wow, you'd think they would have kicked us out or something," Veronica said. "Good company." Veronica gave Mel a quick hug. "Let me take you home. We both have to work in the morning."

Mel groaned, "Thanks for reminding me."

When Mel entered her condo, she could see the message light on her answering machine flashing. She clicked the play button to hear the one message she received. "Mel, I don't think you're being fair. I didn't know Tonya was going to be at the party. She surprised me. I went to the party looking for you. Don't you think we should talk about this? Are you willing to throw what we have away over someone you don't know and someone who could care less about me? I told you I love you Mel, and I mean it. I won't call you anymore. Call me if you want to give us a chance."

Mel played the message a couple more times thinking it over. She didn't want to throw their relationship away. She thought about what Veronica said, how she was tired of the club scene. She was too. She wanted to hang around home more. She wanted to have someone to come home to at the end of the work day. She wanted to go somewhere on the weekends with the person she loved. Could she trust Reggie? She started to think about how Tonya was holding on tight to Reggie, but was Reggie holding Tonya tightly? Maybe it was so that he wouldn't drop her. He did seem surprised to see her. Mel found herself picking up her cordless phone and dialing Reggie's number.

"Mel?" Reggie asked sounding surprised.

"Hi, Reggie."

"I didn't know Tonya was going to be there. Veronica said she ran into Tonya at the mall one day and ended up inviting her. I wasn't planning to crash the bachelorette party. The guys were so bored and disappointed that I didn't hire strippers or anything, so that was the only thing that I came up with. If I had known what showing up to the party would have cost me I wouldn't have gone. I'm sorry. Okay, I'm sorry. I don't want anything to do with Tonya; you have to believe me," Reggie said all of this in a rush and in one breath. Afterwards, Mel could hear him taking deep breaths.

"Reggie, okay, I believe you," Mel interrupted his quick rambling. "I'm sorry for jumping to conclusions."

She heard Reggie let out an intake of air, "Phew, thank you."

"So what have you been up to lately?" Mel asked conversationally.

"Besides worrying and stressing over you, just working. What about you?"

"Same."

"Oh," they were both quiet for what seemed like minutes but was only a couple of seconds.

"Would you like to go out on Friday?" Reggie asked eagerly.

"Sure," Mel said wondering if she let Reggie off too easily.

"Okay, I'll pick you up around six thirty."

"Okay," Mel said.

Chapter Six

As promised, Reggie picked up Mel at six thirty on Friday. He asked her to dress semi-formal. So she wore a little red sleeveless dress and black pumps, light makeup with red lipstick and left her hair curly. "You look beautiful," Reggie said as he held the door open for her as she slid into the passenger seat of his Corvette. He wore black dress slacks and a white button-down shirt. He was clean shaven and must have had a fresh haircut. Mel fought the urge to wrap her arms around his neck and kiss him when he slid in next to her in the driver's seat.

"So where are we going?"

"To a little sushi place. I hope you don't mind," Reggie answered

Mel made a face, "I never had sushi before."

"You'll love it. If you don't, I promise to take you somewhere else to eat afterward." He crossed his heart.

They were both quiet during the twenty-minute drive to Westlake Village. The restaurant was located just off the waterfront. Lights reflected off the water, and they could hear little flaps of water. They were seated outside on the patio. Mel refused to eat uncooked fish, so Reggie was forced to order only items that were fried or baked. "You know you aren't eating sushi if it's cooked, right?" Reggie asked with a grin.

"Yep, and it's fine if we keep it that way," Mel said. "Sorry to burst your bubble but I just can't go there, okay?"

Reggie grinned again and held his hands up, "Okay, I'm not going to argue with you."

"So have you heard from my cousin at all?" Mel asked.

Reggie shook his head, "Nope. I guess they are having too much fun in Cancun and don't want to pick up the phone to tell anyone they made it there okay."

"If I were them I wouldn't want to talk to anyone on my honeymoon either."

Reggie nodded, "Yep, I'm with you on that. We are going to be all to ourselves on a secluded island somewhere."

"Yep," Mel said before realizing what she just said. Reggie grinned.

The waiter appeared with two glasses of saki. "To new beginnings," Reggie said holding his glass up. Mel held her glass up as well and clicked his. They each took a sip.

Mel took a gulp then said, "Oh, it's beer." She grinned approvingly.

Reggie laughed, "It's more of a rice wine."

"You and your wine," Mel complained, "and stop laughing at me. I told you I've never been out for sushi."

"You're so funny Mel. You don't realize it."

"Yeah, I'm Lucy Ricardo in disguise just a darker shade."

"Yep and Veronica is Ethel."

Mel couldn't help but laugh at that.

Mel's laughter subsided, and she looked a little serious, "Reggie can I ask you something?"

"Of course," he said before taking another sip.

57

"Why didn't you mention Tonya was white? I mean I know it shouldn't matter, but it does."

He sighed. "Yep, it mattered. Her father put a lot of pressure on her when we were dating. She cheated on me a lot, but he was the one who broke us up."

"Really?"

"Yep, she wanted to make her dad happy, so she broke up with me."

"Wow," Mel frowned.

"And before you let the thought enter your head. I am over Tonya. I don't have any unresolved feelings for her. She lost me when she cheated on me and completely lost me when she caved into her father. I lost respect for her a long time ago. I can't be with someone I don't respect."

Mel nodded.

The waitress appeared with Mel's fried Salmon wrapped in rice and seaweed. Reggie had eel and oysters. He tried to convince Mel to try some, but she wouldn't budge.

"I have to admit that a part of me feels as though I'm letting you off the hook too easily."

Reggie nodded, "I can understand that. I was trying to imagine if the tables were turned, how I would react to you being in an embrace with one of your ex-boyfriends. I probably would be sitting in a jail cell."

"Really?" Mel asked.

"Really. I don't think I could handle you being with anyone else."

Mel raised her eyebrows in surprise.

"Why do you seem so surprised? You still don't believe how much I care about you?"

"I don't know Reggie. I mean we've seen each other for over nine months. Sure to some people that is a long time but I still feel like there is a lot that we still need to get to know about each other. I know there is still a lot that you don't know about me and my past. I don't know if I am comfortable enough with you yet to share it."

"Yeah, but I feel like I've known you forever. Maybe it's because I've known Terrence for over a decade and a half."

Mel nodded, "I mean, yes, a lot of times I do feel like I've known you forever too, but that doesn't mean that I do. You know what I'm saying?"

Reggie nodded. "I guess I do. I hope that you will open up to me and share your past with me soon."

Mel shrugged, "Maybe one day I will."

Two weeks had passed since the wedding, and Mel hadn't heard from either Lisa or Terrence. Finally Friday night Lisa called to announce they were back in town and was having a barbecue at their house the following day. Mel arrived at Lisa, and Terrence's the next day in a gray tank top, black shorts, and black flip flops with silver hoop earrings dangling from her lobes. From the entry way, Mel could see all the way to the backyard patio where Reggie was lazily sitting on a lounge chair with a soda in his hand. He waved to Mel.

Terrence embraced Mel in a hug, "Hey cuz! I feel like I haven't seen you in years. I never see you anymore."

Mel crossed her arms. "You're the one who doesn't bother calling. You always have your wife call me on your behalf. You don't take personal phone calls anymore."

Terrence frowned. "The whole wedding business just took a lot of time. You know that?"

"Doesn't mean you can't be with your family, especially the ones you lived and grew up with."

Terrence looked down at her guiltily. "Sorry, Mel. I didn't mean to be so distant. I was under a lot of pressure."

She gave him another hug. She never could stay mad at Terrence for too long. It had something to do with him standing up for her in elementary school, junior high and high school. She had always been a target for jokes amongst her classmates for one reason or another whether it be her short hair, her tiny little body, her flat chest, her fast walk and faster run... it was always something, but Terrence always defended her. "I forgive you just don't do it again okay? Promise?"

Terrence crossed his heart and said, "Promise."

From the corner of her eye, Mel could see Reggie was trying to get Mel's attention to come outside and sit by him. But before going outside Mel wanted to take advantage of the time alone she had with Terrence even if it was only for a few minutes, "Hey Terrence, can I ask you something?"

He wrapped a muscular arm around her and said, "Anytime, what's up?"

"What are your feelings about Tonya?"

He removed his arms a little too quickly and with a hint of panic in his voice asked, "What... what do you mean?"

Mel ran her recently manicured hands through her curls. "I mean do you think that Reggie is over her? Do you think Tonya is still after Reggie? What was their relationship like? I had Veronica's take on it and even Reggie's but what's your opinion?"

"Oh," Terrence coughed; his light brown eyes seemed relieved. Mel was pretty sure it was one of Terrence's fake coughs he tended to do when he was nervous about something. "Well, you know, they broke up a long time ago. The breakup was hard for everyone. They refused to go anywhere the other would be, so it split up the friends for a while."

Mel shook her head in irritation. "I don't care how it affected the friends. I want to know if it is over between them."

Terrence nodded his head, "Yep, it's definitely over between them. Reggie doesn't have any respect for Tonya."

"So you don't think that I have anything to worry about?"

"Nope," Terrence answered wrapping an arm around her again, "Now, let's go outside and eat before all the food is gone."

"Okay," Mel agreed. When they were out on the patio, Mel took a seat right next to Reggie. He leaned over and kissed her on the lips.

Pablo and Veronica were sitting in lounge chairs close to the table. "Hey," Mel called out to both of them waving.

Both of them waved back but didn't bother to stand up to greet her. They were too involved In a conversation that appeared to be private and in Spanish.

Lisa joined Mel at the table kissing her on the cheek. "So how was the honeymoon?" Mel asked.

Lisa passed Mel a thick photo album that she hadn't noticed on a small circular table. "See for yourself," Lisa said. Her hair was pulled back into a loose ponytail.

"We went snorkeling, jet skiing, went to fiesta's almost every night... the food and alcohol were all inclusive at the hotel. It was so much fun! I didn't want to come back."

Mel noticed Lisa was bright red. "You didn't have any sunscreen."

"Yes, but to get into the water we weren't allowed to put sunscreen on. It's against the law there."

"Really?"

"Yep and we were in the water a lot."

"Except for the beach that allowed us to be in nothing but our birthday suits," Terrence announced laughing wickedly.

"Really?" Reggie asked.

"Oh, yeah, it's nice there," Pablo said.

"Who is he?" Reggie whispered to Mel.

"Veronica's private stripper," Mel giggled back in a little whisper.

"What?"

"Don't worry, he's gay," Mel whispered.

"No way," Reggie said. "He's not gay. He was checking out Veronica's backside when they first walked in, and the guy was drooling."

"Really?" Mel asked loudly.

Pablo and Veronica looked at them.

Reggie nodded confirmation.

"Hmmm… see… he's up to something," Mel said suspiciously.

"Yep, he wants to get laid by Veronica. That's what he's up to."

Mel shook her head and explained quietly, "No, it's more than that. The guy has been meeting with the president of the company that they work for. Don't you think it's strange that a new hire would be meeting with the president of a company?"

"I think we both need to mind our own business. Veronica is a grown woman. She knows how to handle herself."

Mel grunted but didn't say anything further. She continued flipping through the photo album not paying attention to every single picture. At a glance, she could tell Terrence and Lisa had a great time. All of the images that Lisa was in, she was smiling her genuine happy smile.

"Would anyone like a glass of wine?" Terrence asked carrying a bottle of Merlot and a corkscrew.

"Not Mel," Reggie said.

"No thank you cuz," Mel answered ignoring Reggie.

Pablo and Veronica each accepted a glass.

"Wine and ribs, wow," Mel said but everyone ignored her.

Lisa placed a bowl of potato salad on the table and a platter of corn on the cob. Veronica and Pablo had moved to the table to sit with everyone else. Everyone was quiet as they ate. Mel was studying Pablo. There were a couple of times that she noticed Pablo looking to his right where Veronica was sitting and deliberately looking at her cleavage. He wanted Veronica in the manliest way possible. He glanced up once and saw that Mel had been studying him. He gave her a small wicked smile then winked at her. Mel felt herself jump a little from the shock and almost knocked herself out of her seat.

"You okay, babe?" Reggie asked. "The ribs too spicy for you or something?"

"No, it's not the ribs that are spicy," she murmured. She wondered if she should talk to Veronica. She knew she couldn't ask Reggie for advice because he made it clear he wanted to stay out of it. But Veronica had never been intimate with a man; would she know what she was up against? Mel finally stopped arguing with herself and decided that it was her duty as a true friend to Veronica to let her know Pablo was truly up to no good.

"Hey Ladies, when you're done eating can you help me with the dessert?" Lisa asked.

Mel jumped at the opportunity, "Sure, you need help now?"

Veronica sighed, "Do you need me?" She had an arm resting on Pablo's shoulders.

"Yes," Lisa and Mel said in unison as they each got up and headed back into the house.

When they were in the kitchen, Lisa asked, "Veronica, what are you doing? Do you even know him?" She opened the refrigerator and pulled out cans of whipped cream.

"Of course I know what I'm doing. I'm having fun with my friends."

Lisa handed Mel a pie cutter and slid the store bought apple pie over to her on the kitchen island.

"So, you see the way he's been looking at V like she's his dessert for later?" Lisa asked Mel.

"Who could not see it?" Mel responded.

Veronica sat on the stool not helping with the dessert at all. "He's my friend. Stop talking disrespectfully about him."

"V, do you know if he's gay or not?"

"Does it matter? He's turning out to be one of my best friends. He always wants to spend time with me, and I enjoy his company. There isn't any sex pressure with him. I feel safe."

"No sex pressure?" Lisa asked, "He's going to jump you tonight as soon as he is alone with you. I guarantee it."

"Not everything is about sex. Both of you have been brainwashed. You should have been abstinent before marriage. You would see what a real relationship is about."

Lisa slammed down the can of whipping cream, "Really? I don't know what an actual relationship is about?"

"And apparently neither do I?" Mel commented questionably.

"Look, I think you and Terrence were lusting after each other for years. And you are the queen of lust Lisa," Veronica pointed out.

Mel frowned from confusion, "How could Lisa be the queen of lust?" Privately Mel thought Lisa was too serious and rigid.

Veronica's eyes widened, "Oh… you don't know, huh?"

Lisa suddenly looked panicked, "Don't you dare V… I'm warning you… I have whipped cream in my hand…"

Mel held up the pie in her hand, "And I have pie… spill it Veronica."

Veronica smiled wickedly. "I'm more afraid of the pie and Mel combined."

Lisa aimed the can towards Veronica. "I'm warning you one last time."

Mel had her left hand on her hip while the right held the pie aiming it towards Lisa.

"Ah, you don't want to mess up your kitchen. I'm not worried," Veronica said to Lisa then turned to Mel to explain, "Lisa refused to date at all while we were in college. She would get stressed out and super mean during finals but at the end of every year when she took her last final she would go down to the student pub and pick up a guy. She would disappear for the whole weekend. One time she was gone an entire week," Veronica said.

"Are you serious?" Mel asked wide eyed as she placed the pie down.

"I needed release somehow so hooking up with a stranger who was willing to put condoms on for a weekend was a great way to relieve stress," Lisa explained slamming down the whipped cream.

"Wow, you're not as uptight as I thought you were. You're a slut," Mel giggled.

Lisa nervously shifted from one foot to the next. "Hardly, it's not like I did it every weekend. It was once a year."

"But Lisa, you picked them up at a bar?"

"Not just any bar it was the university pub. They were educated men who were just as stressed out as I was. How many times do I have to explain, if they were willing to put a condom on we were good to go." Mel wasn't sure, but she thought she caught a glimmer of a wicked grin on Lisa's face for a moment as she explained her scandalous past.

Veronica shook her head disapprovingly, "That's why I have Mr. Happy. I can't get any diseases or pregnancies from using my vibrator with bunny ears."

Lisa plugged her ears, "I don't need to hear this."

"Aren't afraid you're going to get addicted to it?" Mel asked curiously.

"No, I already *know* I'm addicted to it," Veronica said matter-of-factly.

"But," Mel tilted her head to the side with a confused expression on her face. "Isn't that just as big of a sin as premarital sex, Miss High, and Mighty?"

Veronica became agitated and sputtered of Spanish then switched back to English. "Listen, though, we are completely getting off track of what I was talking about. Sex isn't all there is in a relationship. You have to establish a truly valuable friendship first. You can't just jump into bed with someone when you don't know anything about them. If you can't imagine yourself being the person, you are sleeping with you shouldn't be with them."

"What?" Mel and Lisa said in unison.

"You have to respect the person as a whole. Can you close your eyes and imagine yourself as Terrence and respect him, Lisa?"

"Well, yeah. We are alike in a lot of ways."

"So you've got it then. Mel can you imagine yourself as Reggie and respect him."

Mel frowned then shook her head, "I still have more to learn about him."

"Then you shouldn't be sleeping with him," Veronica said.

"It's too late," Mel said.

"For who? You or Reggie."

Mel squirmed feeling guilty and uncomfortable.

"I'm sorry, I am not supposed to judge. I know that you and Reggie belong together because I know Reggie, and I think I know you, but I wish you waited. Anyway, you do not need to worry about Pablo. We are friends, and I am not sleeping with him. He knows how I feel. I'm waiting until my wedding day."

"Wow," Mel and Lisa gasped in unison.

Reggie walked in rubbing his belly, "I knew you were busy talking instead of dishing. What's for dessert?"

Reggie put a hand behind Mel's neck. Mel felt goose bumps rise on her skin and the butterflies in her stomach, "Apple pie," Mel answered with a croak.

"Hey, you feel a little tense, you okay?" Reggie asked in a low voice close to her right ear. She felt more goose bumps.

He put both of his hands on either side of her neck and began kneading then moved to her shoulder then back to her neck and down to between her shoulder blades. Mel closed her eyes and let out a groan.

"Oh get a room," Veronica said annoyed and walked to the patio.

Lisa giggled and took the pie to dish slices and spray the whipped cream. Mel and Reggie helped Lisa carry the pie and plates outside.

Pablo and Terrence both groaned at the same time. "Yesss, pie!" Terrence shouted as if he won some sort of national championship.

Veronica was sitting next to Pablo again, "Yep, one of my weaknesses. Thanks a lot, Lisa."

"Oh please, like you need to watch your weight," Lisa said as reclaimed her seat next to Terrence.

"So," Veronica said looking at Lisa suspiciously, "Lisa when are you going to make your announcement."

Lisa blushed.

Terrence grinned.

"What are talking about?"

"I have my grandmother's gift. I can tell when someone is pregnant."

"You didn't waste any time, did you?" Reggie asked loudly, not waiting for any confirmation.

"Well, I'm the godmother. You were the maid of honor so that automatically makes me the godmother, 'cause it's my turn and it's only fair," Mel said.

Lisa put her right hand on her abdomen. She smiled, "Well, you all apparently believe Veronica. She's right. I'm only a few weeks. Yes, we had a little head start before the wedding. But we didn't want to tell anyone until after the first trimester. Next time V can you keep it quiet?"

Veronica raised her hands in the air, "What? We are all practically family. We don't keep secrets."

Mel noticed that Terrence squirmed uncomfortably in his seat.

Pablo lifted his forkful of pie and whipped cream and said, "To the new baby and the new parents!"

The others followed and raised their forks.

Chapter Seven

Later that night Mel and Reggie were snuggling in Reggie's bed in Oxnard. A fresh breeze ruffled the light weight curtains from his bedroom window. Moonlight seeped through whenever the curtain raised. The flapping of the waves from the Pacific Ocean could be heard. Mel's head rested comfortably on Reggie's chest. She listened to his heart beat and stroked the patch of hair on his chest. She felt at home.

"Do you think they are rushing it?" Reggie asked breaking the peaceful silence.

"What? You mean Lisa having a baby?"

"Yeah," he stroked Mel's left arm, periodically reaching up to her shoulders and kneading them.

"I do. I think they should get used to being married first before they bring a baby into the picture. But, it's too late to tell them that."

"True."

They were both quiet for a while again but then Reggie asked, "So how long do you want to wait after marriage? Do you want kids?"

Mel shifted a little. She was going to roll over, but he tightened his grip on her.

"We're just talking Mel. Don't panic. Now answer the question." She wasn't sure, but she thought she could hear him smiling. She was too afraid to make eye contact with him, though.

She cleared her throat then answered, "I want at least two kids. I want to keep it at an even number so when we go to an amusement park everyone has a partner for the rides. No one is left out like I was."

"You were left out a lot?"

"Yep. I'm an only child, remember?"

"But you lived with Terrence most of your childhood, right?"

"Half of it... or maybe more than half of it."

"But Terrence wouldn't want you to feel left out, why'd you feel that way?"

"Terrence's brother Greg was cool to me, but his two sisters were always distant. I guess it was the age difference. They're ten and twelve years older than me and were always too busy to do anything with me or invite me to hang out with them."

"So why did you live with them anyway?"

Mel shifted uncomfortably but decided to explain, "I don't remember a whole lot. I know that I was six years old, and it was in the summer that my mom dropped me off. She had Terrence and Greg take me out in the backyard to play while she talked to my Aunt and Uncle. I remember this look on her face. She was so sad and tired. Before going outside, I ran up to her to give her a big hug and kiss. I guess I had this feeling that she was going to take off. Anyway, when I came back inside my aunt and uncle sat me down at the kitchen table for dinner and told me I would be staying with them for a while. I cried and cried because she didn't say goodbye to me the right way."

"Maybe it was too hard for her," Reggie said softly.

"Sometimes I think that but other times I think she just couldn't wait to get rid of me."

"But you don't know why she left?"

Mel shook her head, "Nope."

"Your aunt and uncle didn't tell you."

"I asked them twice. They told me that when she wanted me to know she would tell me."

"That's rough."

"Mean, don't you think?"

"Knowing Terrence the way I do, his parents are probably protecting you."

"You're right, but I'm thirty, I think I have a right to know what happened to my mom."

"True."

They were silent again for a few moments then Reggie asked, "So… even number of kids. I can handle that." Reggie's grip tightened again. "How soon after we get married do you want to have children?"

Mel tensed up. "I don't know if I'm marriage material."

"Well, hypothetically, if you were to get married, how long do you think you will want to wait before getting pregnant?"

"I think a year is good. In fact, I wouldn't mind starting to make a baby on our year anniversary. That would be romantic, don't you think?"

"Yep, I like that. I'd take you to a hotel far away that has a Jacuzzi in our room, room service and chocolate."

Mel grinned despite her slight discomfort, "Now, you're spoiling the surprise."

"Oh, you like to be surprised?"

"As long as it's a good surprise and revolves all around me, yes."

Reggie laughed but said, "Okay, so I will file that away for future. Pretend you didn't hear me tell you about the hotel, all right?"

"Okay."

"So do you care if you have boys or girls?" Reggie asked.

"Nope, I think two kids are fine. I don't think it matters if they are boys or girls. I could have a girl with boyish tendencies or a boy with girlish."

"Oh, no, we aren't having a boy with girlish tendencies, okay? I would not be able to handle it."

"What about Pablo?"

Reggie burst out laughing and coughed, "I already explained to you the man is heterosexual. He and V are probably in bed together right now."

"I somehow doubt that," Mel mumbled.

"Enough with the talking," Reggie said lifting her up closer to him so their lips could touch.

Two weeks went by in a blissful blur. Mel and Reggie alternated which home they would be in, but they were together every day. Mel was surprised that she didn't feel smothered. She couldn't wait to get off of work just so she could spend time with Reggie. The evenings were always too short and she tended to dread the weekday mornings but found herself waking up earlier on the weekends in hopes of having more time to spend with Reggie.

One Saturday afternoon, Mel had her legs stretched out on top of Reggie's on her sofa. The television was on, but neither one of them were looking at it. They were both lost in their own thoughts and feeling lazy. The phone rang. "The phone is ringing," Reggie announced as if Mel didn't hear it and tapped her foot.

"Yep, you can answer it if you want."

"Nah, its way in *your* bedroom."

"It's ok," Mel insisted.

"Nah, I don't want to step on your fear of commitment toes. If I answer your phone, you will think that I think I live here or something."

"It's ok," Mel said again.

Her answering machine clicked on after the fourth ring, neither one of them moved. "If it's important whoever it is will leave a message."

"Yep," Reggie agreed.

They heard Veronica's voice on the machine, "Oh chica! I have to talk to you. Call me as soon as you can. Lisa is freaking out."

"Oh, no," Mel said but still not moving.

Reggie tapped her foot then started shaking it, "Mel, don't you think you should call her?"

"I'm debating. Everything is drama with Lisa. I'm trying to figure out whether it's real drama or just drama drama."

"If it's Veronica calling it has to be real drama," he said.

"True. Can you get the phone for me?" Mel asked overly niccly.

Reggie laughed, "Nah, I don't want to just walk into your room then you will think I sleep there."

Mel hit him. "You do sleep there."

He grinned, "Yeah, I know but you know what I mean."

"Knock it off."

Still they both remained on the couch unmoving.

Her phone rang again this time the answering machine clicked on the second ring. "Mel, it's Lisa, call me, please." She could hear Lisa sniffling.

Mel let out a groan then finally rose from her couch in search of her phone. She found it on her nightstand. She decided to call Veronica first before calling Lisa. Veronica would be able to give her a briefing without tears. "Oh, I'm so glad you called. You won't believe what's been going on."

Mel sat on her bed and ran her fingers through her curly hair. "What happened?"

"Terrence left Lisa."

"What?! Wh… why?" Mel stood up and started to pace.

She heard Veronica take a deep breath. "Well, this part you aren't going to like."

"Just tell me…"

"Okay, I feel like it's all my fault even though I'm not the one with the sperm that made the baby and this is a prime reason why I don't have sex…."

"V, what are you talking about?"

"Okay, I ran into Tonya at the mall the other day. I just bought my new stilettos and I heard her arguing with a little boy. I turned around to see her standing on the escalator and the boy threw some pants on the floor and started shouting. He was saying he didn't want the pants so he wasn't going to try them on. He was really cute and I thought he looked familiar, but I couldn't quite figure out who he looked like. Then I realized that he called her mommy. So I walked over to her and she looked nervous and scared. She actually blushed bright red and stuttered for a moment, but she held the boy's hand. He must be about four years old. He has light skin, curly brown hair, and light brown eyes."

"Mmm hmmm…" Mel said impatiently wondering when Veronica would hurry up and explain what happened.

"Well, I told her we had to talk and asked her to call me later. She didn't call right away. I thought maybe she was afraid. Well, anyway she called me but said she didn't want to talk about it over the phone, but she felt she didn't have much of a choice. To make it short, Terrence is the father."

"What?!" Mel said too loudly because Reggie ended up walking into her room to join her.

"What's going on?"

"I'm talking to V. I'll explain in a little while."

"Oh, chica, you can't tell Reggie yet. He will go after Terrence."

Mel frowned, "I thought you said there weren't any feelings left and I didn't have to worry."

"You don't, but there is a code that Terrence broke. He shouldn't have slept with his best friend's ex-girlfriend... ex-fiancé. What he did was atrocious. How could he do something like that?"

"I don't know but if the boy is four, it was long after the big break-up."

"True but Reggie is intense and protective."

"But if he doesn't love her, he shouldn't care."

"That's not the point Mel. He's going to kick Terrence's butt out of principle. Let's say Terrence and Lisa split up Reggie would never consider dating or sleeping with Lisa because she's marked as Terrence's even after break up."

"Oh, brother."

"It's... it's... ahh... that's the way Reggie is. I know how he thinks."

Mel felt her blood boil. She looked at Reggie, who was now sitting on her bed with his eyes closed. Veronica knew Reggie so well and always seemed to point out how much she didn't know about him. Veronica obviously thought highly of him and would always defend him. "Why aren't you dating him?" Mel found herself asking exasperated again.

"Will you stop it and focus on the situation at hand?" Veronica asked, annoyance in her voice.

"Will you tell me why Terrence left Lisa already?" Mel asked just as annoyed as Veronica.

Reggie sat up, "What?" he asked in a high pitched tone.

Mel waved him away so she could focus on Veronica.

"Well, like I said, I feel like it's my fault. I told Tonya that I would invite Terrence over to my place and she would have to come over and explain to him. I know Terrence would want to know he has a son."

"So I have a new cousin," Mel realized in a daze.

"Yep, he's cute too. He looks a lot like Terrence. I know Lisa. She will eventually snap out of the shock and fall in love with his son too. He's so adorable."

"But why did Terrence leave?"

"I'm getting to that. You keep interrupting me, though."

"Will you just spill it?" Mel had such a tight grip on the phone, her knuckles were turning pale.

"Fine!" Veronica yelled then sputtered some Spanish. Mel was pretty sure Veronica was cursing her out but switched back to English. "Terrence came over and Tonya told him about their son. She showed him a photo album. Terrence insisted they will have blood tests to confirm it. But you can just look at the boy and know. I believe Tonya. But apparently when Terrence got home he told Lisa right away and Lisa went off on him. He just packed a bunch of clothes in a duffle bag and took off."

"This isn't good, V," Mel said pacing back and forth.

"I know. Lisa shouldn't have all this stress right now. We don't want anything to happen to her or the baby."

"I should go over there," Mel said.

"I think that would be a good idea."

"Okay, I'll get a change of clothes and drive over to Lisa's now. I'll call you later, all right?"

"Okay," Veronica said then Mel heard the click of the phone.

Reggie stood right beside her with his arms crossed and a look in his eyes that she knew translated to tell-me-all-now or else. Mel didn't want to find out what the or else would be so despite Veronica's warnings she told Reggie what she knew.

"I don't believe it," he said shaking his head. "I won't believe it until after the blood test." His jaw clenched.

"Why do you want a blood test? Do you think it can be yours?" Mel asked suspiciously.

Reggie looked annoyed, "I know it isn't mine. I haven't been with Tonya in over ten years. You just said the boy is four."

Not realizing she had been holding her breath, Mel let out a sigh of relief.

"Terrence..." Reggie said as if all the information was finally seeping into his mind and soul, "Terrence shouldn't have.... I can't believe.... He..."

Mel noticed Reggie was flexing his fists.

"Are you sure you don't care about Tonya?"

"Of course, I will always care about Tonya Mel! I just know that I am not in love with her! You need to stop asking me about her like that!" Reggie shouted.

"I'm going to keep asking until I get an honest answer. I think you are still in love with her and you are angry with her for sleeping with your best friend even though it was a long time after you two were together."

"I am angry but not in the way you think. It's a matter of respect and trust. I would never date or sleep with any of Terrence's ex-girlfriends or Lisa if they broke up. How could he do this to me?"

"He didn't do it to you. See, you are still connected to Tonya."

"Yes, Mel, I will always be connected to Tonya just as you will always be connected to your exes. You need to trust me, Mel. That's what all of this comes down to. I'm not the other guys you've dated. I'm not the same guy I was a year ago! I don't want anyone but you. You are not going to question my feelings for Tonya ever again, you understand me?"

Mel had never heard Reggie raise his voice to her. He had never threatened her before. Once again, it was one of those do what I say or else type of moments and again she didn't want to know what the or else was. She bit her lip and nodded.

"One day you will open your eyes Melody Roberts and see that I am in love with you and there is nothing you can do about it."

She gulped. She hadn't realized he had backed her up against a wall in her bedroom. She felt the nearness of him and her body was inflamed with a feeling she had never experienced before. She felt as if her soul was entangling with his. His soft full lips met hers and he led his tongue to dance with hers. She felt her eyes moisten.

Finally when she came up for air Reggie's eyes were gleaming and searching hers. She lifted her right hand to wipe away a tear then cleared her throat. Mel shifted slowly away from him and she said, "Well, I have to check on Lisa. I'm going over to her place now. You can stay here if you want. Just lock up if you go anywhere."

"Okay, I might go home tonight. Who knows, maybe Terrence is waiting at my place right now."

"That's a good idea," she said, but she doubted Terrence would show up at Reggie's. She knew Terrence would probably avoid Reggie as much as possible.

Chapter Eight

Mel was sitting on Lisa's couch rubbing Lisa's back in circular motions to soothe her. Lisa was still sobbing uncontrollably. "Thank...th... thank you for coming Mel."

"You're welcome. I had to be here. I can't believe it."

"Me either. How could they sleep with each other?"

"They probably just connected one day when they both needed to be held. Don't take it so personal Lisa."

"How can I not take it personal? I am supposed to be carrying our first baby only to find out that I have a four-year-old stepson. And if Tonya thinks that we aren't going to be a part of the little boy's life, she has another think coming. Terrence is a good man, he's going to want to know his son and so will I."

"Wow, so if you're willing to accept his son? Why did Terrence leave?"

She nodded then confessed with another sniff, "I pushed him. I was so shocked at first and I was yelling and cursing and throwing things. He said I was controlling and couldn't handle things not going exactly to the way that I planned them. I think he's right, but he didn't have to leave," Lisa blew her nose again into a big wad of tissue.

"Well, I don't think he's gone for good. He probably needs a little time to himself to digest everything."

"I just wish he would call or text me and tell me where he is. I would do that for him if the tables were turned. I would at least tell him where I was."

"Don't worry Lisa, he'll call."

Two days later Mel had just got off of work and plopped down on her sofa when her cell phone rang. It was Terrence. "Where are you?" Mel asked without saying hello.

"I'm at the hotel across the street from the mall."

"Have you called Lisa to let her know you're okay?"

"No," he said, sounding bitter. "I don't even want to talk to her right now."

"Terrence she's your wife and the mother of your future baby. You can't be causing all of the stress on Lisa. She's worried."

He sighed. "Maybe I'll call her later."

"So spill it. How did all of this happen?"

"Thanks for asking calmly. I've needed to talk to someone about this and make some sense out of it, but no one wants to hear me out. They just start lecturing me and asking me if I know how to use a condom."

"Let me guess that was Greg, right?"

"Yep."

"Okay so tell me already..."

"I just got off of work one day and had a rough day at the office so I decided to go to a club. Reggie couldn't meet me for whatever reason, but I ran into Tonya there. She was out with a couple of her girlfriends. She was having a bad day too. We started talking and of course drinking and by the end of the night we were both too drunk to drive. We could have called a taxi or had one of her friends come back to the club and take us home, but we opted to stay at a motel. It started off strictly platonic. But when she came out of the shower she was so breathtaking. Mel..." he paused sounding as if he were in pain.

"Go ahead, I'm listening," Mel said encouragingly.

"I... I never felt like that with anyone since... not even Lisa. It was so intense between us that night. We talked and then the passion we felt..."

"Oh boy..." Mel sighed.

"Yeah, oh boy is right. I've tried to forget that night. I love Lisa, but Tonya was so easy to be with. She's special. She laughs and smiles and doesn't take life so serious. She just lives. She always has. I've always had a crush on her but didn't do anything because Reggie asked her out first before I even had a chance. Before... before I could even tell him that I was into her."

"Oh..."

"The next morning Tonya told me we shouldn't have slept together and that it wouldn't happen again. She didn't want to hurt Reggie any more than she already had. So I agreed to try to forget about it."

"Oh."

"So here I am sitting in a hotel room six years later hiding from Lisa and Reggie."

"So you admit you're hiding?"

She heard him let out a snort. "You know Reggie is going to hurt me, right? Don't ever tell him I said this but I am scared of him. I never want to be on the receiving end of one of his punches. And Lisa... Lisa is way too emotional right now. I can't cope with my own emotions in addition to her drama."

"Lisa is your wife. She is supposed to be an anchor for you. She told me she wants to be a part of your son's life and that she has forgiven you already. She admitted to pushing you. But you know what Terrence? You can't be selfish right now. You can't just walk away and not face all that is your responsibility. This isn't just about you and Tonya. This is about your son, your wife and the circle of friends that surround you. I know you didn't mean to hurt anyone, but you did and you have to face it."

He groaned, "Not you too?"

"Yes, I agree with Greg but I'm not going to lecture you, Terrence. You have always been ahead of this whole life game. I've always looked up to you and respected you. I think you already know what you need to do, but you are just afraid to do it. But suck it up! Call your wife! Call Tonya and arrange for Lisa to meet your son. Then you will have to face Reggie but you might be right in waiting a while for that one. I think he still has feelings for Tonya."

"Stop saying that. He's over her. He loves you."

"Then why did he ball up his fists so tightly and the vein pop out in the middle of his forehead when he found out about you and Tonya."

"That's simple. He probably thinks that I slept with her while they were going out, but I didn't. I only slept with her once and that was a long time after they split up."

"I'm not convinced. You should have seen him, Terrence. You would think they were still going out or something." She needed some sort of tangible proof of how he truly felt because words weren't enough. Words were easily lies. Her gut was telling her Reggie wasn't over Tonya, no matter what anyone else said.

Terrence sighed heavily, he sounded as if he was carrying the world on his shoulders. "Do me a favor, call Lisa and tell her where I am? Let her know I love her but I just need some time to myself to process everything. I need to think. I can't do that with her yelling at me."

Mel knew she should refuse, but she knew that if she didn't give Lisa the message he still wouldn't call her and she'd be worried. "Fine, but don't avoid her for too much longer, okay?"

"Okay, thanks," Terrence said before hanging up.

Mel slid to a laying position on her couch and stared at her smooth ceiling. Why couldn't life be smooth like that? Things didn't really have to be so complicated, did they? When she thought about it, it really was simple, wasn't it? So what Terrence had a baby with Tonya? So what there was a four-year-old son in Lisa and Terrence's life, an unexpected surprise? She wondered how her aunt and uncle viewed her arrival on their doorstep. Did they see it as a new complication or an unexpected surprise? Her aunt always did her best and tried to fit the maternal role that Mel needed. Her uncle was hardly ever home so she really wasn't that close to him even though he was her mother's brother. She wondered if he was out of the house so much because of her or if it truly was because of his job. She felt a tiny lump forming in her throat and her eyes were beginning to sting with unshed tears.

She said a prayer for the little cousin she hadn't met yet and for the one Lisa was carrying. She prayed they'd both grow up to be confident, strong, happy, and healthy secure individuals. She prayed that Tonya's son would never feel abandoned but loved. She would have loved to have her father enter her life at any age.

If she unexpectedly got pregnant, would Reggie be a permanent fixture in her and the baby's life or would he run? She prayed she'd never have to find out. She wanted to get married first before having a baby. But she would wait until she was secure in the marriage before she brought a baby into the picture.

She reluctantly dialed Lisa's phone number and passed on the message from Terrence. Lisa sounded relieved to know that he had finally made some sort of contact and agreed she'd leave him alone and let him come to her. Mel didn't know if she would be that calm if it were her in Lisa's shoes. Mel would have bullied who ever knew where her husband was into telling her where she could find him then beat the crap out of him for hurting her so bad. That could be why Lisa was in management while Mel wasn't. Lisa was mature and sophisticated and could handle anything that came her way.

"Hola Mel, what are we going to do today? Let's have some girl time."

Mel smiled at Veronica's perky voice on a Saturday morning two weeks later. "You know what V, I am so ready to have some fun. Reggie is working all weekend so what do you want to do?"

"Hey, that's not fair, I asked the question first," Veronica giggled. "This reminds me of my teenage years when I would sit on my dad's car in the garage and stare at my friends during the summer. We would be bored out of our minds and keep asking each other what are we going to do? We always thought once we made money we would be having fun all the time. But... look at us.... We sit on the phone and ask.... What are we going to do? My teenage self would be so ashamed of me as an adult."

Mel laughed. "Let's play tennis."

"Heck no. I am not chasing after a ball and getting all sweaty. Try again."

"Basketball?"

"Did you not just hear me chica? I said I am not chasing after a ball and getting all sweaty."

"So you aren't chasing after Pablo?"

"Stop it."

Mel tapped her fingers against the kitchen counter top. "Let me guess… shopping… to the mall we go…"

"Now you're talking. I'll pick you up in thirty minutes?"

Six hours later Mel returned home to find Reggie sitting on her couch watching a Laker game. Mel blinked not sure if it was her imagination or not. "Hey, Mel."

She wondered if she walked into the right condo because he had never been in her condo waiting for her before. She wondered if maybe she somehow ended up at his house by accident. She looked around the condo… it was hers. She dropped the one bag onto her coffee table. The bag contained an oversized t-shirt that she planned to use as a night shirt. "I thought you said you had to work all weekend."

"I do but only half days. I missed you so I thought I would surprise you. I knocked a bunch of times, but you didn't answer so I used my key."

"Oh," Mel said still standing by her door.

"Why didn't you just call me?"

"Because I wanted to surprise you."

Mel crossed her arms. Something wasn't right. Reggie never just appeared without calling her first. "Reggie you've never just come over unannounced before and you've never used the key before. What's going on?"

"I told you I just felt like surprising you. Is that a crime?"

Something inside of Mel shouted *yes, it was a crime.* She wasn't sure she was in the mood to argue with him. He seemed down. In fact, his mood kind of killed the perky buzz Veronica instilled in her all morning and afternoon. Mel sighed and resigned to curling up next to Reggie on her couch. She rested her head on his shoulder and he wrapped an arm around her. He planted a kiss on her forehead. "I missed you. Don't freak out just because I was in your place without you. I just wanted to be with you. I didn't want to drive all the way back to my place. Besides, I knew the Laker game was starting and you know I can't miss my game."

Mel relaxed a little bit. "Okay, I'll let it slide this time."

"Why did you give me a key if you don't want me to use it?"

"I don't know. I just did. Let it go, okay?"

"I will for now. But I'm filing it away for a future discussion when we start arguing about why you'll eventually marry me. But we aren't having that discussion yet because I just want to watch the game with the woman I love sitting right next to me."

"Fair enough," Mel agreed.

"Um..." Reggie grinned, "Do you have some popcorn and beer?"

Mel rolled her eyes but went into the kitchen to pop him some popcorn and grabbed a bottle of beer from the refrigerator.

Chapter Nine

A few weeks slipped through the cracks of time, Mel and Reggie were in mutual neutral contentment. No pressures, no worries. Veronica appeared on Mel's doorstep one Thursday evening knocking frantically on her door. "Chica, something is definitely up with Pablo," Veronica explained as she dropped her enormous purse near Mel's front door. "Today I walked into the office and he was talking to the Vice President of the company in a low conversational tone. When I came up to say hello to them, Pablo told the VP that he would call him later so they could discuss the proposal in more detail in private. The VP looked at Pablo as if *he* was the boss or something and he looked scared of Pablo. What was that all about? I asked him and he said I'm imagining things. Then... you know what he did?"

Mel frowned but asked, "What?"

"He smacked my behind and then squeezed it."

Mel's mouth dropped open, "Did anyone else see in the office?"

"No. We were the only ones left in the room. Then guess what he did?"

Mel raised a quizzical eyebrow.

Veronica's face flushed as she confessed, "He kissed me. Not on the cheek and not one of those quick, friendly kisses he usually gives me. He gave me a full blown I-want-you-bad on the mouth tongue dancing kiss. He didn't stop there Mel. He kissed me more and grabbed my cha cha's." Veronica grabbed her own breasts for emphasis.

"What did you do?"

"I lost my mind and forgot who he was and kissed him back. I'm scared Mel. He's my best friend, but he's been lying to me. He led me to believe he's gay, but I don't think he is. If the cleaning lady hadn't walked in on us I might have done the horizontal mambo with him, you know? I don't want to lose it with him again. I want to be married, I told you that. How could I lose it like that so easily?"

"Have you really looked at Pablo? You do realize he's all testosterone and you are a full grown woman, right?"

"You know what I mean Mel," Veronica's eyes misted over. She made the sign of cross then kissed her thumb. "Ay, what do I do?"

"Why not try talking to Pablo?"

"I guess I have to, but I'm afraid to be alone with him now."

"Well, call him."

"He'll only say it's all in my imagination."

Veronica followed Mel into the kitchen and sat down on a stool. Mel's elbows rested on the countertop while her chin rested in her palms. "Let me guess, you want me to talk to him."

"Will you, please?"

"What do you want me to ask him?"

"I want to know why he's been meeting with upper management and what's the big secret? I want to know if he is gay. I want to know why he's playing with my mind, emotions and hormones."

"So, you are attracted to him?" Mel asked with a smile.

"YES! Hellooooo, haven't you been listening to anything that I'm saying. Mel, I was about to get butt naked in the office! I'm not like that!"

Veronica's hands were shaking and her eyes were misting over again. "Okay, I'll call him." Mel reached for her cordless phone and asked, "What's his phone number?"

"You're going to call him *now*?" Veronica asked excitedly.

"Yes, what's the number?"

Veronica gave her the number. Pablo answered on the third ring. "Hola?"

"Um, Pablo?"

"Yes," he said.

"This... this is Mel."

"Oh, Hi Mel. How are you?"

"I'm okay. Thanks. Veronica asked me to call you. She's sitting her next to me and she's kind of shaken up."

"Oy, did I come on too strong today? Let me talk to her."

"I will but I want to ask you a few questions first and please be honest with me. Okay? Veronica is one of my best friends now and I don't want her to get hurt. There is no way to ask this than to just ask it. Are you gay?"

Pablo laughed a deep rich laugh, "No." He laughed more, then admitted, "I started the rumor at work."

"What?" Mel asked astounded.

"I started the rumor."

"Why?"

"Because I didn't want to be pestered by all the women at work. So the very first day at work when one of the women asked me out on a date I said I wasn't interested because I was gay."

Mel laughed and continued laughing even though Veronica was sitting in front of her with an enormously confused frown on her face.

"So why lie to V?"

"I didn't lie to her. I just didn't correct her assumption. I don't know Mel. I guess I just liked to hang out with her, but then she became one of my best friends and then she is so sexy, you know? She is so beautiful, especially when she is mad and suspicious. She puckers up her lips without realizing it and well, she did that today when she saw me talking to Ron and I just had to kiss her, you know?"

Mel cleared her throat, "I don't know about all of that... but I'm guessing Ron is the VP."

"Ah, yes."

"Okay, so why have you been talking to the upper management and keeping secrets from her?"

He sighed, there was a long pause before he said, "Mel, that is something that I want to tell her face to face and in private. Between you and I right now, I hope to explain everything to her after she accepts my marriage proposal. I can't explain it to anyone before then."

Mel's mouth dropped. "Well, when do plan on that?"

"What? Proposing to her?"

Mel looked at Veronica to see if she caught on to any part of their conversation. Fortunately by the expression on Veronica's face, she still appeared to be confused. "Yes," Mel smiled.

"Well, I'd like to take her to the beach this weekend and tease her senselessly until she begs for me to take her but I won't because I know how much she wants to wait until she's married. So I plan to dangle the ring in front of her, she won't have any other option."

Mel giggled. "I like that."

"Me too."

"Well, good luck with that. Would you like to talk to her now?"

"Yes, thank you."

Veronica looked flustered, "What did he say?"

"Sorry, can't tell you," Mel said as she handed Veronica the phone.

Veronica narrowed her eyes at Mel but snatched the phone from her. She immediately began sputtering off quick Spanish into the phone and got louder and louder with each new sentence. Veronica's eyes started to redden and tears were beginning to stream down her cheeks. Veronica's conversation ended with her saying, "Adios!" She clicked off the phone then slammed it onto Mel's counter top.

Veronica rushed to the front door and picked up her purse and pulled her keys from her pockets. "I have to go. I... I hurt Mel. I have to go." Mel wanted to console Veronica but didn't think anything she said would help her. She wished she could tell her what Pablo's intentions were. He loved Veronica, but he was hiding a lot from her. No one could clear that up except for Pablo. Mel gave Veronica a hug. "Are you sure you're okay enough to drive V?" Mel asked.

"Yes, I'll be okay. I just need to be alone. He lied to me. He keeps lying."

Veronica sniffed and opened the door.

"Call me when you're ready to talk, okay?"

Veronica nodded then was out the door.

Chapter Ten

Reggie took Mel to the movies that Saturday night and they went out for ice cream afterward. As they were walking out of the parlor, Lisa and Terrence were walking in. They were holding hands. Mel felt the tension in the air shift immediately. Terrence stepped back a few steps just as he recognized Reggie. Reggie's jaw tightened and Mel could see the muscles in his jaw flex. Reggie ground his teeth.

"Hi," Lisa said perkily. She was wearing a pastel blue t-shirt that said, "Baby On Board" with an arrow pointing down to her belly. Her hair was pulled back into a ponytail. She looked happy. Too bad the men were tense.

"Reggie, I...."

"I think you need to stay away from me," Reggie said.

"Can't we get passed this in some way, come on, Reggie, you have Mel. Why does it have to be complicated?" Lisa asked still smiling.

Reggie flexed his jaw again, his nostrils flared. "Lisa, this is between me and Terrence. Stay out of it."

"No," Lisa said as she let go of Terrence's hand and stood right in front of Reggie. Her face only inches from his. "I'm tired of people telling me to stay out of it. I'm sick of being dismissed like a little puppy. Let me tell you something Mister Reginald Dempsey. I am in it. I am in the middle of the muck and let me tell you something. Get over yourself. You and Tonya had problems. Terrence had a crush on Tonya way before you started dating her. He said that a long time ago before you asked her out. Did you ever stop to think that you hurt Terrence first? Did you stop to think about the way he used to look at Tonya or were you too self-absorbed just as you are now?" Lisa's head was moving side to side and she was now pointing a French manicured finger at Reggie. "You need to stop thinking this is all about you and look at all of the people involved. You need to see the full big picture and stop thinking that you are Mister Perfect. If you love Mel as much as we all believe you do, you will get over it and except Terrence's son into the family as I have. And we are all family. You are planning to marry Mel right?"

Reggie's fists were balled, but his jaw relaxed. He blinked his eyes and they softened with each passing blink. Finally, his fists relaxed as well. He began chewing on the side of his cheek.

Terrence's eyes were popped out of his head and glazed over. "Um," Mel sputtered, "um… Lisa, are you okay? You're horribly red."

Lisa blinked and stumbled. Reggie and Terrence reached for her simultaneously. Each grabbing one side of her waist and hand. "Baby, are you okay?"

"I think I need to sit down. I feel dizzy."

Mel pulled out a chair and Lisa sat down. Mel hit both Reggie and Terrence on the arms. "Both of you go outside and talk, now." It was Mel's turn to clinch her teeth.

Mel asked the sales clerk for a cup of water then rejoined Lisa at the small circular table. Mel noticed how puffy Lisa's hands looked. "I haven't seen you in a long time. How far along are you?"

Lisa took a sip of the water and closed her eyes. "I'm thirty-four weeks."

"Geesh, I didn't realize it's been that long."

Lisa nodded in agreement, "Yep, the baby will be here soon."

"Have you been going to the doctor regularly?"

"Come on Mel, you know me," Lisa rolled her eyes, "Mrs. Anal Retentive. Of course, I have. My blood pressure has been a little on the high side. I'm probably not supposed to have ice cream right now but I really, really want some." Lisa grabbed a stack of napkins from the napkin holder then started fanning herself. "I'm so hot. Will you tell Terrence to get me some mint and chip already? Geesh."

Mel peeked out the window just in time to witness Reggie planting a solid punch to Terrence's gut while at least ten onlookers surrounded him. Mel took a deep breath in and slowly let it out. A few people immediately reached for their cell phones. "Crap," Mel mumbled. She really wanted to curse but for whatever reason Veronica's voice seemed to be inside her brain telling her not to. "Lisa, I need to check on the guys. Will you be okay?"

Lisa made a face and continued to fan herself with the napkins. Her other hand rested on the top of her belly. "Fine."

Terrence made his way to sit at the edge of a fountain and was coughing. Reggie, on the other hand, was walking fast in the parking lot, rushing towards his car. Obviously leaving Mel to figure out her own way to get home. "Drama, drama, drama," Mel said as she sat next to Terrence and began rubbing his back. "Just breathe cuz. It will pass."

"The cops are their way," a young man with pimples and glasses said as he shifted nervously from one leg to the other. His hair was down to his shoulders and his legs were skinny and scrawny in tight form fitting jeans.

"Why did you call the cops?" Mel asked.

"Did you see the dude that hit him? He looked like he wanted to kill him."

"He did, but he won't," Mel said, "Come on, let's get Lisa and go before the cops come. We don't need more drama, okay."

Terrence nodded. He seemed to finally catch his breath. Lisa came wobbling out of the ice cream parlor with a small cone in her hand. "I'll drive," Lisa said a little too calmly.

"No, I will drive," Mel argued.

"Look, I'm pregnant, not disabled. Don't argue with me. I need any kind of control I can get right now, okay?"

Mel figured she didn't have time to argue with her. They managed to get into the car and drive out of the parking lot before the police arrived. During the drive to Terrence and Lisa's house, it began to really sink in that Reggie had ditched her. Reggie managed to punch her favorite cousin in the stomach and run away. Maybe they should have waited for the police, she thought bitterly.

Lisa was steering the wheel with one hand and munching on her ice cream cone with the other. Her stomach only inches from the steering wheel. Terrence finally stopped moaning as Lisa pulled up in front of Mel's condo. "Are you two going to be okay?"

Terrence was still massaging his stomach but nodded and managed a smile. "Did you see the way my wife stood up to the Raging Reginald? I think we'll be fine."

"Why are you smiling?" Mel asked in amazement. The goofy look on Terrence's face always made her laugh.

"He's gonna talk to me soon. The worst part is over. He hit me now he's just got to talk to me and forgive me."

Mel shook her head and grabbed her purse as she climbed out of their car. "Men." She slammed the door then walked over to the passenger seat and leaned inside to kiss Terrence's cheek, "Cuz, don't force Lisa into early labor with all of this drama, okay? Have you noticed how swollen her hands are?"

"You should see her feet! It's weird. She's thin and regular in the morning but by night time she's puffy like a marshmallow."

Lisa punched him in the arm.

"Ow!" Terrence rubbed his arm, "Well, it's true Lisa."

"I don't need to hear it," Lisa was cranky now, so much for the smiling and glowing person that initially greeted Mel in front of the ice cream parlor. Lisa had finished her ice cream cone and wiped her hands with one of the many napkins that were stuffed in her purse. She wiped off the steering wheel too. Lisa finally made eye contact with Mel. "Now, don't be mad at Reggie for ditching you. Don't add to the drama with more drama."

Mel wanted to say, *look who's talking* but decided to keep the peace instead for now. Anyway, Mel hadn't yet decided how she should feel about Reggie's actions. She figured she'd be able to think it over when she was in the confines of her condo. Alone.

"Well, I'll stop by and check on you more often Lisa. When is your last day at work?"

"I have a doctor's appointment this Thursday. I should know then."

"Okay, love you both. Drive careful Lisa."

Mel reached into her jeans pocket and pulled out her keys then made her way to her condo. She knew Lisa would not drive away until she saw Mel safely inside her condo. Her answering machine was flashing with three messages. She dropped her purse and pressed the play button. Reggie's voice was flat and sounded tired, "I'm sorry Mel. I didn't mean to leave you, but I was afraid if I stayed I would have kept hitting Terrence. I don't know what came over me. Honestly, I thought I could handle it. I mean I knew I was still angry and hurt but..." There was a beep then the next message played. "It's still me. I was saying I knew I was still hurt, but I didn't think I'd hit him. You know. I thought I was passed it. I mean I love you so why should I have this feeling like I'm jealous or something, you know? I don't know where this is coming from. I think... I think... Mel... don't be mad, okay? But I...." Mel sighed as another beep beeped, but Reggie continued onto the next message, "I think I need to talk to Tonya. Not just call her but see her. I just need some kind of closure, you know? Don't think that I love her, because I don't. Well, I mean, yes I love her but I'm not in love with her. I'm in love with you Mel. Believe me. Okay? You're gonna be mad so I'll give you some space. Call me when you're ready to talk. Okay? I love you, Mel." Then there was a click.

Mel felt the pressure in her throat rise and it tried to make it to her eyes to cause tears, but she fought it with all of her might. She wasn't going to waste tears. Mel agreed with Reggie on one thing. She needed space. Everyone seemed to come to her with all of their problems and issues, but no one appeared to ask her how she was doing. Why was that? Did they just assume she was care free and no worries, no problems? For a brief moment, she wondered if Pablo was able to propose to Veronica today as he had planned. Was it romantic? Did she say yes, and if she did say yes, why hadn't Veronica called her yet? Veronica was lucky. She was secure and confident. Mel, on the other hand, didn't really know how others could care about her. Her own mother didn't want to be around her so why would Reggie want her? She wanted to be that confident and strong independent woman but in reality she was needy. She needed to know if the person she was with was truly in love with her and only her. She needed to trust the person completely and right now she didn't trust Reggie. She didn't know if she ever could. Competing with his past was growing tiresome.

On Thursday evening, Mel had just settled down to eat a cup of soup as she curled up on her couch and clicked on the television when her cell phone rang. She glanced at the caller id and said, "Hi Terrence, how's Lisa?"

"She's on bed rest until delivery."

"What? Why?"

"She has toxemia, but it's too early to have the baby. Her blood pressure is way too high."

"You know why it's high, don't you?" Mel said accusatorily.

"Yes, Mel. I know. It's my fault. I don't want her to meet my son until after the baby comes. I don't want Lisa anywhere near Tonya either."

Mel snorted.

"What, what was that snort about?"

"Why don't you tell that to Reggie? Apparently he needs to be with Tonya."

"What? What do you mean?"

Mel sighed then explained the message Reggie had left her.

"Mel, stop reading too much into Tonya. Reggie is over her."

"You want him to be over her, Terrence, but I know he isn't. I know he isn't completely with me. His mind always drifts to Tonya and until he gets her out of his system the two of us can't be together. He thinks that I am the one that needs to call him when I'm ready, but the truth is; he needs to call me when he is prepared to be with only me."

She heard Terrence sigh.

"Look, things may be hunky dory for you and Lisa and Veronica and Pablo, but they aren't peachy for me and Reggie, okay? That's just the way it is."

"Wait, Veronica and Pablo? What are you talking about?"

Mel filled Terrence in on the conversation she had with Pablo. "I haven't heard from V at all. So I don't know if they even got together this weekend or if he actually proposed to her."

"Well, I'm sure she would have called Lisa if he did. She would have told me. I haven't heard anything."

"So maybe…."

"So maybe things aren't so hunky-dory for Pablo and Veronica either."

Mel sighed.

"Why are you comparing yourself to everyone else anyway? What's really going on Mel?"

"I don't know Terrence. I just feel so alone lately. I'm supposedly in this serious relationship with a guy who keeps saying he wants to marry me but more than half the time he's thinking about his ex-girlfriend. I've also been wondering what…" She stopped herself and stared at the television, wondering if she could possibly put her feelings into words.

"What Mel?"

"Do you know where my mom is?"

"Wow, I…. I…"

"Come on Terrence, you have to know something?"

"I'm sorry. I don't know. I asked my mom a couple weeks after you started staying with us and she told me it was grown up business and I needed to stay out of it."

"I think I need to ask your mom again. I mean how old do I have to be to be considered a grown up. I deserve to know the truth."

"Well, call her."

"I will." *When I get enough courage,* Mel thought. "I'm sorry Terrence. I had a little self-absorbed moment. Let me know if you need any help. Do you need me to stay with Lisa at all?"

"Maybe for a few hours this weekend, if you don't mind. I have some stuff to do at work plus I want to spend a couple hours with Jared."

"Jared? Who's Jared?"

"My son."

"Oh, right. Duh? Okay. When do I get to meet him anyway?"

"Well, I'd like to introduce him to Lisa first before the rest of the family. But it will be soon. Maybe a month. Is that okay with you?"

"Yep, as long as it is before Christmas."

Mel visited with Lisa over the weekend and every day after work. Lisa was miserable. She kept trying to talk Mel into picking up her laptop from work so that she could at least get some work done while she was "under house arrest." She simply informed Lisa that she refused to partake in any form of conspiracy that could cause her to go into premature labor and thus Terrence forbidding Mel from ever being allowed to enter her home again. Also, she reminded Lisa that it was against human resource policy to attempt to take another associates laptop, especially when said associate was in management and on medical leave… maternity leave at that.

Lisa crankily replied, "Why don't you just leave then? Have you ever thought that I would forbid you from stepping foot into my home because you refuse to assist me in my time of profound boredom, isolation, and uselessness?"

Mel rolled her eyes and crossed her arms. "Have you ever thought that maybe I wouldn't want to come back here again until after the baby finally comes out?"

Lisa pouted, "I'm sorry. I know we keep having the same conversation every day, but you understand, right?"

"Yes, Lisa, I understand. Well," Mel sat on her bed and changed the subject, "have you heard from V? I haven't heard from her in a while."

"No, I haven't. I miss her. Terrence told me about Pablo. I hope he comes clean with whatever it is that he is up to. Veronica deserves to be treated like a queen."

"I think all of us do," Mel added.

They chatted for a while longer then Mel eventually left to go home. During the drive home, her mind drifted to Reggie. He kept his promise about giving her space. He hadn't called, text, left a message…. Nothing. She felt that emptiness inside of her again. She kept telling herself that she was a strong, smart, beautiful woman who deserved to be treated like a queen. Reggie wasn't ready to treat her the way she should be treated.

Chapter Eleven

Finally a week later Reggie called her on a Friday evening, "You just weren't going to call me, were you?"

"I didn't think I was the one who should call. You were obviously the one who needed space and you knew exactly where I've been. So talk to me..."

"Can I come over?"

"No."

"Ouch."

"Talk. Tell me what you've discovered about yourself during our space and more." She wanted to know whether or not he met with Tonya. She just didn't want to say her name at the moment.

Reggie must have known what she meant because he said, "Well, I did meet with Tonya and I told her how angry and hurt I was to find out about her son." He sighed a heavy sigh and explained further. "I also needed to understand how she used me being black and her father's racism as one of the reasons for not marrying me but then she has another black man's baby. Then, of course, the man just happens to be my best friend." She could visualize him rubbing the back of his neck from thoughtful frustration. He cleared his throat then continued, "She explained that it really was as Terrence said. It was only one night and it was a long time after the two of us split up. She said her father is still as racist as ever but has grown to love Jared."

"And do you believe her? Does that make a difference? About Terrance hooking up with her after you two broke up?" Mel asked plopping herself down onto her sofa and lying down to stare up at her ceiling with a burgundy throw pillow beneath her head.

"Yes, I believe her and yes it makes a big difference. Before I talked to her, I kept wondering if Terrence had been one of the guys who had slept with her while we were engaged. I felt hurt Mel. I felt a burning betrayal I've never felt before."

"And this is supposed to help the two of us how? You were jealous and angry over an ex-fiancé Reggie. How is that supposed to make me feel?"

"What you have to understand is that it wasn't about the two of us at all. It was about me and Terrence."

Mel smirked.

"Believe me Mel."

She smirked again.

"I know you are making one of your smirking faces, but I know you believe me too."

She rolled her eyes.

"And don't roll your eyes either."

She sighed. "Reggie...."

"Mel, I feel like we just keep arguing over stupid stuff. I don't want to argue anymore and I want to spend some time with you. Can I pick you up?"

"You know, Lisa was right, though."

"Huh?"

"The day at the ice cream parlor when she went off on you and almost passed out..." Mel tried to remind him.

"About what?"

"You do get really self-absorbed at times. Everything about our relationship is about you. What you are dealing with, the restaurants you want to try... you want popcorn, you want beer... you..."

"What? Where is this coming from? Popcorn and beer?? What the heck are you talking about?"

"See, you don't even listen when people are talking to you and you have a tendency to interrupt me and others when they are trying to get a point across."

"You know what Mel. I'm tired of being pushed away. I'm sick of the battles."

"See... I'm not finished yet..."

"Well... Mel... this time I am. This time... you call me when you are ready to apologize."

Mel heard a click on the phone. He hung up. She couldn't remember him ever disconnecting her like that. She blinked and kept her ear to the phone just to make sure he really did hang up and not getting back on the line. Finally, she heard the dial tone to confirm that he truly did hang up on her. She sat up and slumped on the sofa. Her condo was too quiet and empty. She didn't want to wait for her mind, body and soul to feel the same way as her condo. She needed to get out.

She dialed Veronica's number. When her voicemail came, Mel said, "Hey V, I don't want to stay home tonight. I'm going to head over to the club on Hillcrest. Don't worry a couple of girls from work invited me earlier today. Meet me over there if you can. I'll be there around nine."

Mel entered the club wearing a tiny black dress and black stilettos. She found three of her co-workers huddled around a small round table in a corner above the dance floor. She gave each of them a hug and immediately stopped a passing waitress to order a lemon drop- vodka, lemon juice, and sugar. Less than five minutes after she arrived, Veronica entered the club holding hands with Pablo. Mel waved her over.

The club was getting crowded and louder. The dance lights were on and it seemed darker than when she initially walked in. Veronica hugged her, "Hi, I've missed you."

"Yep, I missed you too. So what's been going on?"

Veronica grinned bigger than she had ever grinned before and Pablo's hands were around her waist protectively. Veronica raised her left hand. At first all that Mel noticed were her perfectly manicured hands with red nail polish but then the enormous diamond ring on her finger caught her attention. Pablo grinned.

Mel's jaw dropped. "You..." she pointed an index finger from Veronica then to Pablo, "you two are..."

"Si, we're engaged!" Veronica laughed.

"Holy crap!" Mel embraced Veronica in another hug and reached for Pablo to hug him at the same time. They both laughed.

"You have to tell me all about it."

"Oh, you know I will. I just don't want to tell you about it here. We can go shopping tomorrow and have lunch."

The waitress came back with Mel's drink. Veronica asked what she was having then ordered the same. Pablo ordered an imported beer. "So where's Reggie?" Veronica asked glancing around the club.

Mel took a swig of her drink. "He's wherever he wants to be and that's not with me."

Veronica frowned disapprovingly.

"Look, let's just dance and have some fun tonight, okay?"

With that, Pablo held out his hand to Mel and led her to the dance floor. They danced to a hip hop song. When a salsa song came over the speakers Veronica interrupted Mel, "Okay hoochie mama, back off, it's my turn." She giggled. "Let's show them what we've got baby," she said to Pablo.

Pablo immediately spun Veronica in a perfect spin then dipped her, tossed her back up then forced her close to him. Their hips swayed in synchronization to the beat of the music. They shimmied their shoulders, did more spinning and more provocative movements. The entire dance floor dispersed so that everyone could watch them and cheer. The dance ended the same way it began with a spinning dip then sealed with a passionate kiss. The disc jockey cleared his throat then said, "Ladies and gentlemen, give a hand for Veronica and Pablo!"

Mel recognized the disc jockey's voice, it was Mack. Veronica stood and was surprised to see Mack but waved to him.

"Oy, where did he come from?" Veronica whispered as they headed back to their table where their drinks were waiting for them. Mel stopped the waitress again and ordered a reflll.

One of Mel's co-workers said, "Hey, now I know where I know him," pointing to Pablo. "He used to strip at that club in Hollywood a few years ago." A couple of the other girls murmured their recognition as well.

"Yes, the keywords are- used to- he doesn't anymore," Mel said protectively. She was surprised how much she felt the need to protect both Veronica and Pablo.

"Don't worry Mel, it's all good!" One of the co-workers said with a giggle. "Come on ladies! We are never gonna dance if we wait for any of the loser guys here to ask us. Let's take over the floor with our beautiful, bodacious bods! Let's dance. Come on Mel!"

Mel headed back out onto the dance floor as the latest hip hop song blasted over the speakers. At first they had formed a circle of only women but as the dance floor filled up the circle turned into a soul train line. Someone shoved Mel to go first. She shook her butt as she stepped her way to the end of the line. Her heart slammed in her chest when she saw Reggie shaking his groove immediately after her. "What the…"

He was grinning by the time he reached her and kissed her as soon as he was at her side. "Shhhh…." He said. "Let's just have some fun tonight."

She guessed Veronica told him where she was. She'd deal with her later. Surprisingly, Mel just grinned back at him. They started to bump each other's hips to the beat of the music while they waited for their turn to go back down the soul train line. Mel looked around for Veronica and Pablo, but they were nowhere to be found.

Mel woke up in Reggie's arms in the middle of his living room. They were both stretched out on the plush gray carpet between his glass coffee table and fireplace. Her head pounded and her tongue felt like cotton. She put a hand to her head and groaned. Reggie stirred a little then fluttered his eyes open. He mimicked her groan and placed both his hands on his head. She peered at him through tiny cracks from her eyelids. He was naked. She turned to look at the rest of her body and realized she was naked too.

"Do you have any diet Coke?" Mel gasped.

Reggie plugged his nose. "Phew…" he waved his other hand, "baby, your breath is kickin'."

Mel plugged her nose and made a gagging sound. "Yours is too."

He laughed but finally answered her question, "You know I have a stash of diet Coke just for you. It's in the frig."

She slowly got to her feet and made her way to his kitchen. She found the soda on the second shelf. She grabbed one for herself and one for him. He followed her. He grabbed the cans from her hand and popped them both open. He handed one back over to her. She took a swig and closed her eyes. "Ah...."

"Still hurts, though," he whispered after he took a sip as well.

"You know we are going to talk, right?" Mel asked.

"Yes, but let's wait until after the pounding in the heads stop."

Mel drank more soda then said, "Agreed."

"What time is it anyway?"

Reggie pointed at his state of the art microwave. "Ten twenty-eight A.M."

Mel was surprised. She rarely slept in. "What time did we get home last night?"

"You mean this morning? I think it was close to two."

"How'd we get here? We were both too drunk to drive."

"One of your co-workers. She said she lived out here in Oxnard and could drop us off. You were all for it."

"Right," she vaguely remembered taking a shot of Patron Tequila right after her buddy offered.

"I don't want to do this anymore," her stomach was feeling queasy.

"What?"

"Clubbing and drinking too much."

"Me either," Reggie admitted. He had a hand on his stomach and was making a face that said he wasn't feeling good either.

"I need fresh air or I'm going to hurl," Mel said as she rushed to his sliding door to his balcony. He rushed to grab her. "Just don't go all the way outside because you're still naked."

"Oh, right," Mel said. She slid open the door both the glass and screen door and stuck her head out. A cool breeze hit her face. "Ahhh... much better."

"Don't be selfish, move over," he said. She stepped aside making enough room for him to stick his head out as well. "Ahh... that does feel good."

"Well, we had fun, though, didn't we?" Mel asked.

Reggie nodded, "Yep."

"So maybe we just shouldn't drink so much but we can go out dancing every once in a while, right?"

"Yep."

Mel closed her eyes again savoring the breeze again. The queasiness seemed to subside. "Let's go lay down in my room. No hanky panky.... Just sleep."

"Okay," she said. He reached for her hand and they strolled into his room. He turned his ceiling fan on then they both climbed into his king sized bed. They leaned the pillows against the shiny black headboard. "Do I get to keep my bed when we get married?"

Mel yawned, "Yes but not the dark headboard. We'll get an oak headboard."

"What's up with you and oak?"

"It's a beautiful wood plus it's strong and sturdy."

Reggie yawned. They both drifted back to sleep in each other's arms.

An hour later Reggie woke Mel, handing her cell phone to her. "It just started vibrating."

She glanced at the caller ID. It was Veronica. "Hey V," she said perkily feeling better with only a slight hint of a headache.

"Did you forget our shopping and lunch date chica?"

"Oh..."

She heard Veronica gasp, "How could you forget me, Mel?"

"I'm sorry! I just woke up... again..."

"Oh... Long night huh? You can thank me later for tattle tailing on your behind."

"It wasn't like I was doing anything wrong, geez. I was just dancing."

"Yes, but you were dancing without your future husband."

"Don't go there," Mel said, sat up and yawned. "Can you pick me up? I don't have my car. Oh and then you'll have to drive me back to the club to pick up my car."

"Humph... fine. I guess you're in Oxnard at Reggie's then?"

"Yep."

"Okay, does he need to get his car too?"

"Yep."

"Okay, I'll pick you both up but tell Reggie he isn't invited to the shopping. It's just ladies."

Mel looked over at Reggie. He laid down again and had an arm covering his eyes. "I don't think he will mind."

"Good. I'll be there in an hour," Veronica said before disconnecting the call.

Mel let him sleep a little while longer. She ventured into his bathroom. As she stepped into his shower, she recalled the way he had hung up on her before she decided to go out the previous night. For now, she'd keep the peace but they would talk.

Chapter Twelve

"So what are you doing for Thanksgiving?" Veronica asked as they walked through the mall.

"I'm probably going to my aunt's house."

"Oh, you mean Terrence's mom's house?"

"Yep. What about you?"

"I normally fly out to Florida and go to my sister's house, but I don't feel like dealing with her and my other sister this year. I think I'm going to go with Pablo to visit his uncle."

Mel frowned, "You don't get along with your sisters?"

Veronica sighed, "I love them. They are twins and seriously, they are supermodels. They are superficial and competitive. They always remind me how I disappointed my mother."

"What do you mean?"

"Oh, let's find a place to sit down and talk. Let's have some coffee," Veronica suggested.

"Mmmm... coffee... sounds like a plan," Mel smiled in agreement.

They walked into a coffee shop on the second floor of the shopping mall. Once they had their coffee, they opted to take a seat on a couch outside on the balcony. "So… you were saying you disappointed your mom."

"Yes, I did. My mom wanted me to follow her footsteps and be a dancer. She trained me since I was two years old, but it wasn't my dream. It was hers. Anyway, when I was in high school, I enjoyed my computer class so much that I decided I wanted computer science to be my major. My mom was so upset. I don't know if she ever forgave me."

"Isn't it usually the opposite? The whiz kids often want to do the artsy majors and end up disappointing the parents?"

"You'd think. But I was a really great dancer."

"You still are. Look at what happened last night at the club with Pablo! You cleared the dance floor and turned it into a stage. People would pay good money to watch people dance the way you two did."

Veronica blushed.

"Which reminds me…. Tell me the scoop on Pablo… your…" Mel cleared her throat with exaggerated loudness, "fiancé."

"Oy, so much to tell you…" Veronica took a sip of coffee. "Well, he called me and left messages right after I last saw you. You know the day I went to your place and you called him?"

Mel nodded. She motioned her hands to encourage her to continue.

"I avoided him all weekend. I dreaded going into work the following Monday. As soon as I walked into my office there was a bouquet of red roses on my desk with a card. It said, 'The owner of the company requests the honor of your presence to a private lunch to discuss future endeavors which he hopes you agree to be a part of.'"

Mel's eyes widened, "Wow." She took a sip of coffee then said, "That must have been overwhelming."

Veronica grinned but held her hand up. "It gets better."

"Okay, go on…"

"So I didn't know who the owner was or where we were supposed to have lunch. I wondered what Pablo would think. Then I got mad at myself for caring. Then I glanced around the office and didn't see him anywhere. I just wanted to forget about everything and get to work. So that's what I did. Anyway, around twelve thirty my office phone rang. This man told me my driver was waiting for me in front of the building. He told me to grab all of my belongings because I would not be coming back to work."

"That's kind of creepy though too… isn't it? I don't know if I would go."

"Exactly. So I sat there for a while debating whether or not I should go. It's not like I could peek out a window without them seeing me to see who he was. But there was a buzz in the air around the office. I didn't talk to anyone that morning so I didn't think anyone knew what was going on, but I guess whoever brought the flowers into the office caused the rumors. Well… I decided to do what the man had said."

Mel's eyebrows raised in surprise.

"As soon as I was outside, I tried to look into the limo to see who was in it. But, whoever it was deliberately sat close to the driver so that the only way I could see him was to get inside."

"That's creepy."

"Yep, but the curiosity got the better of me. So… I got in."

"And??"

Veronica smiled, "You won't believe it."

"Who was it?"

"Pablo."

Mel almost dropped her coffee. "Wait, but I thought you said you were training him."

"I was. I just didn't know he owned the company."

"What??"

"I know crazy, right? He owns all the companies nationwide and in the process of expanding overseas."

"How could he hide that from you? Why would he have you train him?"

"Oh, Mel, I asked him the same thing. I'm pretty sure I was yelling at him before we pulled out of the parking lot. He refused to get anywhere near me during my tangent".

"So... wait..." Mel held up her hand, "was he ever really a stripper?"

"Exactly what I asked him. I had tears in my eyes from anger for the lies, but he said yes, he really was a stripper. He used his money to get through college. He has an MBA Mel. There I was talking down to him on a daily basis and he has an MBA."

Mel raised her eyebrows again.

"He invested his money and slowly built an empire."

"So what... why did he have you train him? Why the secret meetings? Why didn't he come clean a long time ago?"

"He was scouting out new management for a new office. He liked me from the beginning. He said he kind of got distracted from his goal and wanted to get to know me better. He also told me that he started the rumor about being gay. He didn't want a bunch of women to go after him."

"Wow," was all Mel could say. She drained her coffee then leaned back on the sofa. She kept opening her mouth then closing it. She glanced at Veronica. Veronica was examining her engagement ring.

"I still don't believe it, Mel," her eyes glistened. Veronica's voice cracked as she said, "I found my soul mate."

"But why did you let him off so easily? I mean, he was deceiving you the whole time."

"Oh, Mel, I didn't let him off easy. I demanded the limo driver to stop and let me out of the car. I was going to call you and see if you could pick me up. Pablo told the driver to stop the car then ran after me when I got out of the car. I told him not to follow me and to leave me alone."

"What'd he do?"

"Followed me," Veronica laughed. "I was pretty angry at the time, but now I can laugh about it. He kept quiet but was jogging right next to me while I was trying to get away from him. He knew I couldn't get very far in stilettos."

Mel felt the need to rub her feet from visualizing the pain.

"I was so frustrated, but finally I ended up sitting on a bench in front of an Antique store."

Mel waited for her to continue.

"Pablo sat with me for a little while and still was quiet while he tried to catch his breath. He attempted to reach for my hand, but I moved away from him. I finally looked up at him and he looked so sad Mel. Finally, he told me he was sorry for lying but he didn't think of it as lies. He thought they were omissions that he could fill in at any time. Of course, I told him I didn't trust him. I didn't know him. He knew everything about me... my secrets, my family secrets, my desires, my hopes... everything. He finally grasped just how betrayed I felt. He told me he would be honest with me from that day forward and promised not

116

to withhold any information about anything. He said he loved me and didn't want to go anywhere without me. He said I was his best friend."

"Aw…" Mel said and put a hand over her heart. "That's so sweet."

Veronica nodded in agreement. "I was so depressed when he told me that though Mel. I felt so confused at that moment. I wanted to believe him. I wanted to rush into his arms and stay there forever, you know? But he lied. I didn't know if I could trust him. I think he knew what I was thinking because he told me he'd have the driver drop me off at my place. He'd have someone deliver my car back to my place and to take a few days off of work. He wanted me to take a few days to think about him and what we mean and then he'd take me out to dinner to talk when I was ready."

Mel nodded in agreement, "That sounded nice and fair."

Veronica bit her lower lip and nodded in agreement too. "Yes, but I was still so mad. Anyway, to make this short and quick. I was depressed for those few days and I avoided everyone. I'm sorry for that by the way. But you understand why, right?"

"Yep," Mel said.

"Well, finally I called him up and we went to dinner. We talked and talked and talked. He told me so much about himself. He does a lot for the community and for children's hospitals. He had a baby sister who passed away from leukemia when she was eight." She placed a hand over her heart. "Oh, chica, can you imagine that?"

"I know… it's hard to lose someone you love," she said, thinking of her mother.

"Anyway, we saw each other every day for a while. Then, last weekend while we were in Santa Barbara he proposed to me."

Mel smiled.

"But I'm making him take this gaudy ring back, right after the wedding."

"What? Why?"

"Did you not hear what I just said? It's gaudy and ridiculous! I feel ashamed wearing something so expensive. I told him I only want a simple gold wedding band just like my mama and grandmother. He finally agreed but said it will be a thick gold band."

"So if you don't like it, why are you wearing it?"

"Pablo insists I wear it because he wants all the men in the world to know I am already taken."

Mel rolled her eyes, "Men."

Veronica finished off her coffee then glanced at the time on her cell phone. "Thank you for shopping with me today Mel."

"Thank you for inviting me. I'm really happy for you and Pablo."

"Yep, oh..." Veronica said as if she just remembered something. "I haven't told you the big part. We are getting married in Hawaii in a couple of months. I'd like for you to be my maid of honor."

Mel blinked surprised, "Hawaii... maid of honor?"

"Yes, aside from Pablo, you're one of my best friends."

"Thank you V."

"You're welcome. Don't worry about the finances. Pablo promised to fly you and Reggie out along with Terrence and Lisa too."

"Wow. He's really that wealthy?"

"Yep," Veronica said with a frown.

"Why don't you seem happy about that?"

"It's scary. I don't know how to feel about marrying a wealthy man. I never even dated someone who made more than I did, but now I'm going to marry someone who has way too much. I just don't know if I can live up to expectations or anything."

Melody waved a hand, "V, you're starting to make excuses. Stop it, okay. You two know each other now. You can handle anything. You are one of the smartest, beautiful and strongest woman I know. Stop worrying, okay?"

"Thank you, Mel. So, you'll be my maid of honor?"

"Yep, absolutely."

Veronica let out a joyful yelp then reach over to give Mel a hug.

"Now, we need to think about Lisa. She needs a baby shower ASAP. How about next weekend?"

Mel bumped her forehead with the palm of her hand. "I'm a horrible cousin. I didn't even think of that."

"See, that's why I'm going to be the baby's godmother," Veronica teased.

Mel put her hands up, "Uh huh, we already had this discussion. I'm the godmother for this one. You can have the next one."

"Hmmm… Knowing Tonya… Jared probably wasn't baptized yet. So I have dibs on Jared."

Mel blinked for a moment then pouted, "But then you will be the godmother of Terrence's first born."

Veronica put her hands on her hips. "Yes, but you will be the godmother of Lisa's first born. Chica, you can't be the godmother to everyone. You have to share."

"I can't believe we are arguing about this. Fine. You're Jared's godmother since you've already met him and I haven't even met him yet… even though he's got some of my blood running through his veins."

"Hehe… gracias," Veronica grabbed Mel's hand and pulled her off the couch, "We've chatted for too long. Let's get some shopping done. We can go get some baby clothes and decorations for the shower."

Chapter Thirteen

Surprisingly everyone who was invited to the baby shower was able to make it on such short notice. They decided to have the shower at Terrence and Lisa's house since Lisa was restricted from moving too much. She sat on a couch in the living room with her feet up on an ottoman. Mel thought Lisa was glowing and so much more beautiful than she'd ever seen her. Terrence insisted it be a couple's shower so all of the guys were there as well. The house was filled with guests.

Reggie had stayed close to Mel throughout the shower. She realized she still hadn't had the conversation she'd wanted to have with him and it had been nagging at her more lately. *Maybe tonight*, she thought.

"Hey, Mel," Terrence's mom sat in a chair next to her. "How've you been? I haven't seen you in a while."

"Hi Auntie Jane," she reached out to give her a one arm hug with her right arm. "I know. It's been a busy few months." She looked at her aunt. Aunt Jane's skin was light like Terrence's. She was slim and a few inches taller than Mel. She wore mascara and light brown lipstick that matched the light brown blouse she was wearing. Her dark brown hair had a strand of gray and was pulled back into a curly ponytail.

Aunt Jane put her left hand on Mel's knee, "Well, I must say you and Veronica did an excellent job of putting this shower together on short notice. The decorations are cute and I can't wait to eat the cake. I hope it's as good as it looks."

Mel smiled. The cake was shaped like a baby carriage. The bottom layer was chocolate, the top layer was white, and the filling was raspberry with whip cream which was Lisa's favorite. "A friend from work offered to make it. Lisa use to be her boss."

"That was sweet of her. So... do you think Lisa will be going back to work after the baby is born?"

"A part of me can see her plugging her laptop in the day she gets out of the hospital. But I get the feeling once she sees the baby she will want to take a lot of time off."

Aunt Jane nodded, "I agree."

Mel glanced down and fidgeted a little with one of her silver bracelets.

"So Mel, what's on your mind?"

Mel looked up in surprise at her.

"You always fidget when you want to ask me something but not sure if you really want to ask."

Mel bit her lower lip. "I just don't think this is the right place to ask you what I've wanted to ask you for a long time. It just never seems like there will ever be a good time to ask it."

Aunt Jane looked concerned, "Then just ask me, Mel."

Reggie was close by but chose that moment to walk outside to the backyard where Terrence and other guys were. Terrence was barbecuing hamburger patties, drinking beer and laughing.

"Well," Mel fumbled on her words, "I… I've been thinking about my mom a lot lately. Can you tell me what happened to her?"

Mel looked pleadingly into Aunt Jane's eyes. Mel could see buried pain there that was coming to the edges of her eyes. Aunt Jane blinked her eyes, her voice strained as she said, "I wish I knew honey. I miss her too."

Mel felt a blow to her chest. Someone had to know where her mom was. How could she just be gone without a trace? "Can you at least tell me more about what she said before she left that day?"

Aunt Jane nodded. "Yes," she swallowed and reached for Mel's hand to squeeze it. "Do you remember you had a broken arm that day?"

Mel's eyes widened then she frowned, "No."

"You had bruises on your face and legs too."

"What?"

"I still don't know all that happened to you. The day she brought you to me I made up my mind you were staying." Aunt Jane was still holding Mel's hand. "My sister-in-law was heavy into drugs and had been with the wrong people ever since high school. That day she told me she wanted you to have a better life. She wanted to give you a chance and wanted to try to straighten herself out. She said if she ever got sorted out, she'd come back for you. Your uncle had a hard time seeing his sister fall apart, but he had more difficult time seeing her drag you down with her. We agreed it was best for you to stay with us."

Mel's throat tightened. She was finding it hard to breathe.

"So you don't remember anything about the time before she dropped you off."

Mel remembered when she first arrived at Aunt Jane's house her cousins looked at her with fear in their eyes.

Aunt Jane only told them to take her to the backyard and play while she talked to her mom. Later she remembered going to a hospital and being examined by a doctor. The doctor put a cast on her right arm and gave Aunt Jane a piece of paper. Now she guessed it was the prescription for pain medication. But Mel didn't remember any physical pain.

Aunt Jane took a deep inhale of breath then a slow exhale out, waiting for Mel to say something.

"I don't know. I mean. I just remember this feeling of knowing it was going to be the last day I would see her. It's hard to explain."

Aunt Jane reached over and gave her another hug. "I wish I could tell you more, but I haven't heard from her since."

Mel nodded sadly.

Just then Veronica walked into the room carrying three rolls of tissue paper and announced, "Okay, gather around everyone. It's time to guess how big Lisa's belly is. Take a roll of tissue and guess how much is needed to wrap around Lisa's waist to her belly button." A few people laughed. Lisa made a face at Veronica that screamed I'm-going-to-hurt-you.

Mel swallowed her hurt and resentment. She had to remember she was at a party for a baby and not dwell on her own sorrows. Aunt Jane patted her hand and seemed to be thinking the same. "Let's get back to the shower, shall we?"

Mel forced a smile and nodded, "Okay."

Mel reached out to Veronica and grabbed a roll of tissue. "I want to guess. I know I can't win a prize, but I'm not passing this one up."

Veronica giggled.

There was a knock on the front door. Someone who was standing close by answered it. Mack walked in holding a baby gift bag and looked rushed. Veronica looked surprised and frowned, "Mack..." she whispered, "what is he doing here?"

Mel looked concerned and rose from her seat to stand next to Veronica. "Hey, Mack, what's going on?"

She could tell he forced a smile on his face. "I wanted to drop off a gift for Vanessa Williams."

"Can you stop calling me that already?" Lisa whined as she rubbed her belly but laughed.

"Lady V, can I talk to you privately? It will only take a minute," he looked pleadingly at Veronica and then at Mel.

Veronica nodded, asked Mel to take over managing the game then walked out to the front yard with Mack.

Mel tried to focus on the party guests and wrote on a notepad how many squares each of the guest's guessed it would take to wrap around Lisa. She kept glancing at the door in anticipation of Veronica's safe return. How did Mack know about Lisa's party? How did he know it would be here at Terrence's house? It was a little more than eerie.

Finally, ten minutes later Veronica re-entered the house. She appeared upset and rushed to the restroom. Mel excused herself momentarily from the party and knocked on the bathroom door earnestly. "V, it's Mel. Open up."

She could her Veronica sniffling from the other side of the door, but she opened the door. "What happened? What was that all about?"

Veronica wiped a tear away with a piece of tissue. "In Mack's words... closure."

Mel rubbed Veronica's back.

"He came by to say goodbye to me. He explained that he really believed that one day I would open up my eyes and see what a great guy he truly was and would eventually marry him. He said he felt like I had lied to him and led him on the whole time. He said he felt used."

"What?"

Veronica shrugged her shoulders as more tears flooded out of her eyes. "I have never led him on. I've always been honest with him, right?"

"Right."

She sniffed, blew her nose then grabbed another piece of tissue to wipe her eyes. "He said he forgives me though because he found his future wife. It turns out his neighbor has always had a crush on him and finally asked him out a couple of months ago. They've seen each other every day since. He asked her to marry him a couple of weeks ago. He said it was the week before he saw me and Pablo at the club. He is mad at Pablo for lying to me. He said he isn't jealous but worried that he may be keeping more lies from me."

"Oh boy," Mel said in a whisper.

Veronica nodded and blew her nose again. She swallowed then asked, "Do you think Mack is right? Do you think Pablo could be keeping anything else from me?"

Mel sighed, "Well... really anyone can keep anything from anyone. It's just a matter of how big that anything is, you know what I mean? Besides you said the two of you talked at length and you feel like you know him, right? I mean before you felt it in your gut that he was hiding something, right? Don't let Mack's anger and bitterness affect what you and Pablo have."

Veronica nodded, "Yes, I know my Pablo," she sniffed and blew her nose one last time. Mel saw her eyes change to something resembling strength and a little bit of anger.

"Ay, I can't believe Mack would say those things to me. I'm so mad at him now." She balled up the tissue and threw it in the trash. She washed her hands. "Oh, chica, look at me. I'm a mess because of him. Give me a minute to freshen up, please. Can you get my purse from Lisa's room and bring it to me? I need to redo my makeup."

Mel did as she asked and quickly handed her purse. She needed to return to the party. *Geesh, what a day of emotional turmoil*, Mel thought. She caught a glimpse of Pablo and Reggie talking outside. They appeared in a deep conversation. Pablo kept rubbing the side of his jaw as if he were thinking about something serious. She wished she could read lips and know what they were talking about. She shrugged her shoulders and figured they were talking about Veronica and the wedding plans. She resumed her focus onto the party guests that were inside playing games.

Chapter Fourteen

Later that night Reggie stayed with Mel at her place. They were both relaxing on the couch. "You know, we never did talk about why you hung up on me and why you showed up at the club."

"I noticed that too," Reggie said, "I was hoping we could leave it alone."

"But don't you think it was significant? You interrupted me when I had a very valid point to make, literally disconnected me then showed up to the club."

"It's only as significant and complicated as you make it, Mel. You and Lisa made your point. I have selfish tendencies and I've been working on them. Why do you think I showed up to the club?"

"Either you were afraid another man would ask me out and I'd say yes or you felt guilty for hanging up on me."

He nodded then admitted, "Yes, maybe a little of both but something else too."

"Hmmm... What?" Mel asked.

"I wanted us to have some fun together. We had both been so uptight and wound up from everyone else's problems I just thought it would be nice if we had a few drinks and shook our butts together on the dance floor."

Mel grinned, "Yep, we needed that. Thanks for showing up. That was awesome."

He smiled. "Thank Veronica for telling me. At first I was mad but then I couldn't blame you. The only thing for me to do was to join you."

"Can I ask you something else, now?" Mel asked.

"Of course," Reggie said.

"Are you and Terrence okay now?"

"I think so," Reggie nodded, "we talked for a while on the phone after I spoke with Tonya."

"So, are you looking forward to our upcoming trip to Hawaii?" Mel asked.

Reggie nodded, "I still can't believe Pablo rolls like that. A private jet, hotel room, food and drinks provided. Geesh."

"Me either, but I am definitely not going to complain."

That night Mel wakened in panic and drenched with sweat. She sat in her bed and glanced at the other side of the bed. Reggie was on his side sleeping peacefully. She was relieved to see him there. The panicky feeling subsided a little and she wondered what it was that she dreamt to make her feel that way. She bravely closed eyes to see if she could remember. There was a shiny object in her dream. It looked so familiar! Light had reflected off of it as it was coming towards her, but she couldn't see the object. She couldn't remember why it frightened her so much. Deciding not to dwell on it and not to wake up Reggie, she quietly slid from beneath the sheets. She wrapped a robe around her, covered her feet with slippers then headed for her kitchen. She decided to fix herself a cup of chamomile tea to soothe her jumpy nerves.

Thursday afternoon Mel had just finished taking her last customer service phone call before her scheduled lunch break when she heard her cell phone vibrating. She slid open the bottom drawer of her desk and reached into her purse for her cell phone. It was Terrence. As soon as she pressed the green button she heard her cousin, "Mel, it's time. Her water broke while she was cleaning the kitchen this morning. Get down here as soon as you can. Can you call everyone else too, please?"

"Are you at the hospital now?"

"Yes, I'm not supposed to be on my cellphone right now but I had to let you know. I have to go. Hurry up and get down here, though."

He disconnected the phone.

It was a good thing Terrence and Lisa only lived a couple of minutes drive from the hospital. She did as Terrence requested and called everyone. She even stood up from her cubicle and announced to her department that Lisa was in labor, several of them worked with Lisa in the past. There were cheers as well as whispers and murmurs. She figured her announcement would soon reach all of Lisa's co-workers in a matter of minutes. She asked her boss if she could leave early since the phones were slow for a change. Her boss was okay with it since Mel never called in sick or ever asked to get off early, plus she was friends with Lisa. The only condition was for her to call her as soon as Lisa's baby was born.

For a long time, Mel was the only one in the maternity waiting room but that all changed twenty minutes later. Terrence's brothers noisily made their way into the room and were arguing who would see the baby first and whether or not it was going to be a boy or a girl. Aunt Jane soon followed then Pablo and Veronica. Lisa's parents arrived as well. "Well, I don't think we all need to really be here yet. This could take hours."

"Yep, but you know none of us are leaving," Terrence's brother, Greg said.

Two hours and twenty-five minutes later, Terrence walked into the waiting room donned in scrubs and a mask. He took the mask off; tears were running down his face. "She gave birth to a baby girl." Everyone gathered around for a group hug. After the hug Terrence said, "The grandma's get to go see her first. You have to wear scrubs, though. Lisa can have visitors in a couple of hours. She needs to rest."

Terrence reached for his cell phone and passed it to Reggie. "Here are a couple of pictures… we are naming her Nicole."

Reggie had his arms around Mel as he looked at the pictures. "She's beautiful man. Can't wait to hold her," he said and handed the phone back to Terrence. Mel rested her head on Reggie's chest. He squeezed her shoulder and kissed the top of her head and whispered, "I love you, Mel."

She felt the warmth inside of her; comfort and security in his arms, a feeling of home. She wanted more of that feeling. She wanted it only from Reggie.

Three weeks later just after Thanksgiving dinner Terrence's five-year-old son was sitting on Mel's lap at Aunt Jane's house. His hair was an inch long with golden curls, thick lashes, and light brown eyes. "Oh, Terrence, he looks so much like you." She hugged Jared for the hundredth time.

Lisa smiled, "Nicole does too. We're going to get family pictures taken at the mall for the Christmas cards next week."

Jared was playing with a necklace around Mel's neck, Mel's cell phone vibrated. "Happy Thanksgiving Veronica," Mel said.

"Guess what?"

"Um… I think I've had one too many glasses of wine to guess."

"You had wine?"

"It was family pressure. So tell me… what am I supposed to guess?" Mel asked.

"Pablo and I set a date. We don't want to wait any longer. So we are getting married in two weeks."

"Two weeks??! That doesn't give us a lot of time. I have to request time off of work and pack and…"

"Get your behind on a plane and go to Hawaii for the first time in our lives…. How can you make up excuses, especially when it's for your best friend's wedding?"

"Did you tell Lisa and Terrence yet?"

"No, I figured you can tell them while I'm talking to you."

Reggie whispered, "Who're you talking to?" He chewed on a carrot stick, "Let me guess… V?"

Mel nodded and announced to him, "She wants us all to be ready to go to Hawaii in two weeks."

Lisa overheard, "What?? Two weeks?? That isn't enough time to plan a wedding. We don't have a sitter for Nicole or Jared."

Veronica must have heard Lisa because she said, "It's a wedding! Tell her to bring the kids." Mel relayed the message to Lisa.

Lisa shook her head in disapproval, "I don't think Tonya will let us take Jared to Hawaii."

Terrence overheard Lisa and said, "Can Tonya go with us?"

Both Reggie and Mel looked at Terrence as if he were crazy.

Lisa's reaction was a little delayed, but finally she said, "Are you insane? We aren't going to allow a single woman join us in Hawaii."

Terrence held his hands up to claim his innocence. "Look I'm just saying we'd have an instant babysitter if she goes plus be able to have a family vacation with both of our kids. I think it would be great."

Lisa looked at Mel. Mel glanced at Reggie.

"It makes sense to me," Reggie said. "I'm okay with it if you are."

"Veronica, can Tonya join us? She could watch the kids so Terrence and Lisa can have some alone time, but yet they can be together too."

"Wow," Veronica said loudly, "I never saw that one coming. That's fine. If my sisters are coming, Tonya can certainly come. Just as long as you're okay with it, Mel."

"You told me I don't have anything to worry about, right?" Referring to Reggie and Tonya's past.

"Right," Veronica said. "Okay, well, I will talk to you all in more detail later in the week. I had better get back to Pablo's family. They are waiting for me to make a toast. See you later." Veronica disconnected the call.

It seemed too easy. How can someone just decide to go to an exotic island on such short notice and accommodate so many people? Once again Mel was doing something that she knew she shouldn't be doing. She was comparing herself to others and wondering why others were so far more financially successful than she was. Terrence, Lisa, Veronica, Pablo, Tonya and Reggie all had the privilege of going to college. She supposed she could have attended as well considering Aunt Jane had offered to pay her tuition. She just had too much pride. She had already felt like a burden on her Aunt's entire family she didn't want to continue to be a burden when she could make her living on her own. She wondered if she went to college what she would have majored in. She wondered what career path she would have chosen.

Chapter Fifteen

Two weeks flew by. On Friday, they all piled into a van and headed for LAX. Their flight was scheduled to leave at eight fifty-five in the morning and would arrive in Honolulu at eleven twenty-five in the morning. They had to rush to a chartered plane for a short flight to Oahu. The hotel where they stayed was right on the beach. Each couple had their own room. Veronica and Pablo had a honeymoon suite. Pablo offered to get Reggie and Mel a honeymoon suite as well, but Reggie's pride would not allow it since Pablo had already paid for the trip itself.

The group was standing in the hotel lobby. "Well, I am going to the jacuzzi right now. My muscles hurt from the long flight. Do any of you want to join me?" Tonya asked. When no one responded, she asked Terrence, "Can you look after Jared for a while?"

"Of course," Terrence answered with a smile. "Lisa and I will take the kids out shopping and meet you back here at six for dinner?"

"Okay, that sounds good," Tonya answered. She grabbed her suitcase and Jared's duffle bag then headed to her hotel room.

"She looks a little depressed," Lisa observed.

Mel agreed then Reggie said, "She probably realized she lost two perfectly good men, but they are both taken now. Are you sure you did the right thing by inviting her?"

Reggie had an irritated expression on his face. "Whose wedding is this supposed to be anyway?"

Mel was starting to feel Reggie's crabbiness rub off into hers. "Veronica and Pablo's! Snap out of it Reggie. I'm not going to stay in the same room with you if you are going to be moody the entire time." Her head was still hurting slightly from the extensions and braids she had added to her hair the day before exclusively for this trip.

Reggie raised his eyebrows, unclenched his jaw, took a deep breath in and out then said, "Sorry, I just should have thought about it more when you were talking to Veronica about it."

"I guess so. But it's too late now so get over it."

Lisa pulled out a brochure and announced, "It says they have a helicopter tour every hour. A friend recommended we call to reserve it a few hours before showing up for the tour."

"Okay," Mel nodded in agreement then suggested, "So let's go upstairs and get settled in our own rooms. Lisa, you call to get the reservation and then we can figure out what we want to do and if we want to go our separate ways for a little while."

"That sounds good," Terrence agreed.

Pablo interrupted, "I'm taking Veronica shopping, up to the room for an hour or... two... or three... then to a private dinner if she doesn't mind." He looked down at Veronica.

Veronica only nodded in agreement. Veronica hadn't spoken to Mel much during the flight. Pablo and Veronica were in their own world during the entire journey to the islands. For some unknown reason, Mel felt her blood pressure going up and crossed her arms. Reggie must have sensed Mel's frustration because he offered, "Mel, let's go upstairs and unpack. Terrence, do you want to meet us down here in an hour? Or do you guys want to go separate ways and just meet for dinner at six?"

Terrence answered, "Yeah, why don't we just split off for a while and hook up at six?"

"Okay," Reggie said to Terrence then looked at Mel. "Let's get my lady upstairs," Reggie attempted to sound cheerful.

Mel frowned but followed him to their hotel room. When they were in the elevator, Mel said, "I can't understand her." Her arms were crossed and she tapped her foot impatiently in the elevator.

"Who? V?" Reggie asked staring up at the numbers as the elevator carried them higher and higher. Their room was on the ninth floor. The room had one king sized bed, a tiny refrigerator, and microwave. The bathroom had a large tub with a shower and two sinks. There was a view of the beach from their hotel room and a small balcony.

"Yeah, ever since she decided to marry him, she hasn't really been the same. She used to be feisty, a fighter and independent. She wouldn't have allowed him to decide what she was going to do. If anything she would have tried to get me, Lisa and her off alone without you men first. I mean... what the heck happened?"

"She fell in love Mel. I mean, think about it. She is in Hawaii with the man she loves. The man who brought her here and all of her friends and family at that... of course she is going to want to do what he wants to do."

As soon as Reggie closed the door and put down the suitcases, Mel began to undress. She announced angrily, "I am crazy in love with you, but that doesn't mean I am going to forget who I am and become this passive little girl.

I am not going to do things just because you want to do them. If I desire to do something, I am going to do it. I don't need permission. Like if I want to throw my man on the bed right now and make wild, passionate love to him, I'm going to. I don't need him to agree to it. I'd make him agree to it!" Mel was completely naked with Reggie standing in front of her.

Reggie grinned and crossed his arms. "So you think that whenever you want to have sex I am just going to comply?"

"Yes, now take your clothes off, get it up, let's have sex and then go see Hawaii," she said, snapping her fingers hurriedly.

Reggie licked his lips. "I don't know if I should. I don't want to be your boy toy. What about when I want to have sex and you don't? What then?"

"We won't be having any sex then."

"See, now is that right Mel? I mean, really?"

Mel started to feel and look cranky, "Look, I'm horny, come on... stop messing around."

Reggie shook his head.

"Oh, give me a break. Guys are always ready to have sex. Women, on the other hand, have to be really in the mood otherwise there wouldn't be any juices flowing and basically it just wouldn't work, right?"

Reggie shook his head and leaned against the wall. "Mel, I don't feel like having sex right now. What are you going to do about it?" He was hiding a smile.

Mel put her hands on her hips. "Man, I am cranky as I ever will be and horny on top of it. Stop messing with me and give me some!"

Reggie shook his head. "Make me," he said with a devilish grin.

Mel moved seductively closer to him and let he cheek brush up against his. She lightly kissed his ear, cheek, and lips. She moved to his neck and sucked until he let out a groan. With her hands, she pulled his tank top off. She licked and kissed his chest. She unzipped his shorts and slid them off of him. Mel grabbed him by the shoulders and made him turn around so that his back was facing the bed. She kissed him on the mouth and guided him to the bed. She felt him rise and knew she had him. She climbed on top of him.

Two hours later Mel and Reggie emerged from their room and took a walk along the beach. Mel was wearing a peach bikini top and tan shorts. Reggie was shirtless and in white swimming shorts. When they were on the beach, Mel wished the beach was secluded because she would have had her way with him again.

They held hands as they walked. They came across a sign which read, "Want to get married? Why not take the dive while diving?" There was a number listed on the sign. Mel's mouth puckered up. Mel grinned and felt an excitement trickle throughout her body and soul.

She stopped their walk and said, "Um... Reggie." She turned to face him and held both of his hands. "What about getting married under water?"

"Mel..."

She took a deep breath and explained, "See, I never wanted the traditional wedding. You know how afraid I am of the whole marriage thing. It would be really symbolic to marry you while we are diving. You said you wanted to go diving anyway so we would actually be killing two birds with one stone."

"The way you rationalize," he said with a smile. He was quiet for a moment but then asked, "How are we going to exchange vows underwater?"

"I don't know. Let's call the number and find out."

Mel pulled out her cell phone from her shorts pocket then punched in then number advertised. As they walked back toward the hotel room she spoke to the woman who answered the phone, "Hi, my fiancé and I were walking the beach and saw your advertisement. We wanted to know how we would exchange vows in the water."

The woman on the other end of the phone explained the process and informed her if they planned on getting married they should make the reservations now. She also stated they had a cancelation which opened a spot for tomorrow at eleven in the morning. The woman explained they would have to take a class early in the morning for diving as well as anyone who wanted to witness the wedding. Mel explained it to Reggie. Reggie nodded in agreement. They took the canceled reservation time slot then left a message for Pablo, Veronica, Terrence, and Lisa.

Lisa was the only one who refused to take the class. She opted to stay on the boat while the ceremony took place down in the water. Veronica was Mel's maid of honor and Terrence was Reggie's best man. Tonya and Pablo were guests. The vows were exchanged on waterproof templates with waterproof ink pens. The water was clear blue-green. Bright orange, red and yellow fish surrounded them. Coral and abundant shellfish were below them. There were a photographer and a videographer taping the whole ceremony. They emerged thirty minutes later as Mister and Misses Reginald Dempsey.

Mel was able to hide the tears she shed using the water as an excuse.

Reggie's hands were trembling. He blamed it on the water too, saying he was cold, even though it was warm.

When they were back on the boat, Lisa asked, "So… how did it go?"

"She's mine," Reggie announced with a big smile.

Mel only took a deep breath to keep herself from passing out. She felt light headed. She peeled off the wetsuit and was grateful she had braids in hair still otherwise her hair would have been a lost cause even if it was covered by the wetsuit. She was starting to feel shaky. She didn't have any jitters before the ceremony, but they were definitely happening now. It was too late to back out of it or run away. She was Reggie's.

Mel felt hollow inside, though. She didn't understand why. She thought once she married him she would feel complete. She figured that she was probably shaking because she still felt empty inside. There was a great invisible weight bearing down on her.

Reggie noticed her shaking. "Mel, are you okay?"

Her lips quivered, "Yeah, I'll be fine," she said quietly.

Terrence frowned. Mel pretended not to notice her cousin examining her.

"Congratulation Reggie!" Tonya said with a big genuine smile.

Reggie swallowed hard and said, "Thanks."

Pablo and Veronica were taking turns describing the ceremony in detail to Lisa. They were both full of energy and excited. Mel noticed Pablo was already getting darker. Veronica looked at him with a sexy smile and whispered, "I just want to tear you apart."

Pablo grinned then announced loudly, "Well, if you don't mind we are going to go back to the hotel to shower and dress."

"Go ahead," Mel answered a little irritably.

It was quiet on the boat until they reached shore. Tonya took Jared and Nicole back to the hotel. Lisa and

Terrence announced they were going to have some time alone.

Mel knew Reggie was troubled by her mood. He didn't know how to cheer her up. Whenever he asked her what was wrong, she would only shake her head and deny anything was wrong. She was quiet the rest of the day. Finally during dinner Reggie asked, "Mel…" his voice cracked a little when his question was eventually spoken, "Do you wish that we didn't get married?"

Mel put her fork down and lifted her head slowly. She swallowed then aid, "Yes." She looked straight into his eyes.

"What?" Reggie asked baffled, stricken with disappointment and disbelief.

Mel frowned and held her hands up and admitted, "But only because I wish my mom were there."

Reggie sighed from relief, "Oh…."

"I didn't know what was bugging me, but I finally figured it out. I just can't believe she's been gone for so long. She hasn't even tried to call me or find me. She knew where she left me, Reggie. Why didn't she ever call me to see how I was or anything? She could have written me." Her eyes began to water. She sniffed then continued, "I'm sorry I am not cheerful and fun loving right now. Lord knows I am so happy to be married to you, but I didn't realize how much I wanted my mom to be here. All this time, I thought I was fine… I thought I was over the fact that my mom would never be here for me. But I'm not. It's not like she died. She just didn't want me anymore and took off."

Reggie got out of his seat and stood beside Mel. He knelt down and stretched his arms out to her. She accepted his embrace and let out a cry. A few people in the restaurant turned and stared at them. Reggie ignored the stares and said, "It's okay baby. I'm here for you. I know you miss her."

"Yeah," Mel said sniffing.

A waitress passed by with a cloth napkin and handed it to Reggie, "Here you go, sir. Is she going to be okay?"

"Yes, thank you," Reggie answered.

The following afternoon Veronica and Pablo were married under a waterfall. They each had written their own vows. Also, something that surprised most of the guests was when Pablo reluctantly removed Veronica's engagement rock and slid a thick gold band in its place. Veronica smiled. Mel thought the whole ceremony was too much like a fairytale for her taste. She preferred her underwater dive matrimonial ceremony to the fairytale land any day, but she had to admit it was beautiful and, of course, a rainbow appeared just as Veronica and Pablo kissed.

During the small reception, she overheard Tonya ask one of Veronica's sisters. "Why did Pablo switch rings? That was really mean of him."

Mel decided to interrupt the conversation and answer the question on Veronica's behalf, "He didn't want to switch it, but Veronica insisted. She feels guilty having something so expensive on her hand. She asked him to return it and donate the money to the children's hospital where his baby sister was diagnosed with leukemia. She asked for a simple gold wedding band in its place. But I guess you didn't have the opportunity to read the engraving?"

Both Veronica's sister and Tonya stood with their mouths open in disbelieve. Tonya fiddled with the diamond earrings that were in her own ears. "Oh," Tonya finally managed to mumble, "No, I didn't know that. What does the engraving say?"

"To my love, my life, my soul, my wife," Mel's eyes unexpectedly filled with water. She wished Reggie thought of that but of course he didn't know they were going to get married during their stay in Hawaii. Maybe he would have thought of something like that had he had the opportunity to.

"Don't tell Veronica I said this but my sister has always had such a beautiful spirit. I love her." Tonya nodded in agreement.

Mel noticed Reggie approach Pablo and Terrence. All three men were wrapped up in a heavy conversation that seemed to halt when anyone else approached them. Mel wondered what the three could possibly be up to but knew it was useless to try to pry information out of them. She knew she would just have to wait and see... Time would tell.

The friends had spent three more days in Hawaii taking tours of the island and a lot of time on the beaches.

Chapter Sixteen

During the flight home, Reggie and Mel decided to make Mel's condo as their home and agreed to rent out Reggie's condo for extra income. It took a couple of weeks to figure out what furniture would stay and which would go for each of them. One Friday night Reggie was laying comfortably on their bed when Mel nudged him, "Reggie, get up. I have to change the sheets."

"Ah, Mel," Reggie whined, "I just took a shower and I'm nice and cozy."

"Yeah, in dirty sheets. Now get up so I can change these sheets." Reggie grunted but did as he was told. He helped her take the fitted sheet off the bed and tossed it on the floor. He watched as Mel struggled with unfolding the clean pink fitted sheet. She shook it several times before it finally came loose. He grabbed one end of the sheet and placed it on the mattress. Mel disappeared for a moment then came back with a plain blue sheet. She shook it a few times then spread it across the bed.

Reggie crossed his arms with a frown on his face.

Mel looked up and noticed his expression, "What?"

"Don't we have matching sheets?"

"Yeah, somewhere." Mel was too tired to care. She just wanted to sleep on clean sheets.

"Where are they?"

"Reggie, does it really matter?" She asked. Her hair was a mini afro. She had taken the braids out the day they returned from Hawaii. Mel's eyes were slightly bloodshot.

"Yes, it matters. We have matching sheets. Let's match the sheets."

She threw down the sheets she was holding and put her hands on her hips. "Oh, brother."

"Mel, where do we keep the sheets?"

Mel yawned and pointed to the linen closet in the hallway. "I can't believe you don't know where we keep sheets." She vaguely remembered Lisa's complaint about Terrence and towels.

"Don't get wise with me." He opened the linen closet and groaned. He started throwing everything out of the closet and onto the floor. Towels were flying out along with washcloths, pillow cases, sheets and fitted sheets.

"What are you doing?" Mel whined.

"I am organizing this mess," Reggie was naked in the hallway. He separated the towels from the sheets. Then he placed the dark towels on one side of the cabinet and the light towels on the other.

"Isn't that against the law?" Mel asked rolling her eyes.

"What?" Reggie asked annoyed.

"Segregation?"

"Ha, ha... funny... Mel, you've got to start getting organized. One other thing, could you please put the dishes away after you wash them? It bothers me when you keep them out. Why don't you take your clothes out of the dryer after the time goes off too? If you did, you wouldn't have to iron every single morning. Which brings me to another point, you need to stop leaving the iron and ironing board out."

Mel crossed her arms and tapped her foot, "Reggie, don't talk down to me. I am not your little kid."

"Then stop acting like one."

"Oh heck no... I am not taking this from you. This is one of the major reasons I never wanted to get married! I am not going to have someone walk into my life and tell me what to do all the time!"

Reggie put the last towel in the cabinet then said, "Mel, I am not telling what to do. I am advising you what you should do. Something that will make me happy which in turn will make you happy. It will give a sense of order... a feeling of peace."

"Reggie, I don't care if I have mismatching sheets. We are the only ones who will be looking at the sheets. I don't care if there are dishes in the drain board. As long as they are clean and we don't have any company, it doesn't matter. As far as the clothes thing goes... yeah... you're right, if I take them out and hang them up right away, it would cut down on the ironing. The problem is that I simply forget that I have the clothes in the dryer."

"Well," he said with his hands on his naked hips, "start remembering."

Mel sucked in her lips and walked into the bedroom. She reappeared holding a pillow and the blue sheet she had just put on the bed. "What are you doing?" Reggie asked with a hint of panic in his voice.

"Sleeping on the couch. Alone." She passed him up without looking at him. "You can do the dishes from now on. Good night."

"Ah... Crap...." Reggie whispered.

Mel wrapped herself with the blankets and laid down comfortably on the couch. From the corner of her eye, she could see Reggie standing in the hallway. Mel had an enormous frown on her face. "Don't you want to talk about it, Mel?"

"I'm too tired to talk Reggie."

"But..."

"Go to bed and don't forget to turn off the hallway light." She rolled over. Her back was facing Reggie.

The next morning the telephone rang. Mel was still sleeping on the couch. The phone rang again. Mel heard Reggie answer the phone and heard only bits and pieces of the conversation. She knew Reggie was talking to Pablo since he said his name and something about a man named Cedrick. Reggie asked Pablo what he found out and sounded surprised about something then requested an address and phone number. He seemed happy then asked Pablo how much he owed him. Mel rolled over and went back to sleep.

Later that morning Mel heard coffee percolating then smelled the wafting aroma of hazelnut. Her senses heightened from the sound of bacon in a frying pan then of course the smell. Her stomach became alert and forced her to sit up and yawn. She stretched then walked into the kitchen. Reggie was busy in the kitchen fixing breakfast in his robe and slippers. "I didn't mean to be disrespectful last night. I got carried away. I'm sorry. Have some coffee. Breakfast will be ready in a few minutes."

Mel was surprised. "Thank you Reggie."

"You're welcome."

She grabbed a mug from a cabinet, poured the coffee, added milk and sugar then sat at the small table. "So, I would like to take you out tonight, just you and me."

Mel grinned, "Okay."

Mel's hair was relaxed and now had soft curls in her hair. She was dressed in an all-black mini dress and wore two-inch stilettos. She and Reggie had been going to the gym together so her body was much more defined and toned. "So... where are you taking me anyway?" Mel asked for the third time.

"Some place fun. We can eat all we want, dance all we want, have some drinks and then go upstairs to sleep if we want."

"Okay.... a hotel... but where?"

Reggie still wouldn't answer her. He was dressed in gray slacks and black dress shirt. He was clean shaven and doused with cologne and after shave. As planned, they ate dinner at a hotel in Los Angeles which included lobster and shrimp. They each had cheesecake topped with strawberries for dessert. Mel noticed Reggie kept glancing at his watch with his knees bouncing up and down. Mel knew something was definitely up.

"Okay, what's going on here?" Mel finally confronted Reggie.

"Nothing," Reggie asked with his eyes suspiciously wide. His leg started bouncing more. Mel tilted her head to the side. She figured she would let his suspicious behavior slide for a little while. "Let's go dancing," Reggie said nervously to obviously change the subject.

It seemed they had only danced for less than an hour when Reggie glanced at his watch and announced, "Hey, Mel, why don't we go upstairs to our room for a minute. I... I forgot something. We can come back, though."

Mel smirked and put her hands on her hips. "What are you up to? What's going on? You've been acting strange all night."

Of course Reggie denied anything unusual happening. Reggie insisted that she use her hotel key to open the door. When Mel entered the room, there was a light-skinned woman with dyed black shoulder length hair sitting on the bed. She had a few wrinkles around the edges of her eyes and lips. Her eyes were hazel. The woman was breathtaking in Mel's eyes. Something about her though said she'd gone through a lot in her life. A mixture of emotions stirred inside of her: familiarity, fear, love, and fear again. Mel thought perhaps she saw a ghost. She blinked her eyes a few times to be sure she was really there. Finally she asked in an overwhelming whisper, "Mama?"

The woman's eyes began to water. Her legs were shaking. She looked as though she wanted to stand up to greet Mel but was too shaky to move. Reggie reached for Mel's hand and squeezed it tight. Mel placed a hand over her mouth and let out a yelp, sounds from deep within her erupted. Mel couldn't move. She still wasn't sure if her mother was actually sitting in front of her.

After several passing seconds, the woman rose on wobbly legs and stood in front of Mel. She held her arms open to her. Mel flung herself at her mother. They hugged each other tight and cried... and cried... and cried.

"I'll let you have some time alone. I'll be right outside the door if you need me." Reggie said before leaving the room.

As soon as they were alone, Mel asked, "What happened? Where were you? Why did you leave?"

Her mom led Mel to the bed and sat next to her. They held hands. "Mel, I am so sorry. I have said sorry to you every morning and every night in my prayers. I was really selfish and self-absorbed... mostly I was just too young."

Mel looked into her mother's eyes and felt a twinge of disappointment. "Those are excuses... I need you to tell me the truth, the full truth. What happened?"

"The truth…" Mel's mom said sadly. She cleared her throat and said, "It hurts. It's gonna hurt a lot. I'm… I'm ashamed baby girl."

Baby girl… she hadn't been called that since… since… her mom said goodbye.

"Yes," Mel answered looking into her eyes.

"I was only fourteen when I had you, Mel. Your father and I never married. I ran away from home to live with him. When we broke up, I couldn't afford to take care of myself much less both of us. So that was when I dropped you off at my brother's house. My brother was a lot older than me and wasn't messed up like I was. He had never been arrested or anything…"

"You were only fourteen?"

Her mother nodded.

"You never married my daddy?"

"No. He was eighteen as it was. He should have been arrested for getting me pregnant…"

"You said your brother had never been arrested… does that mean you were arrested?"

She nodded and was quiet for a moment. She cleared her throat again. A few tears began to trickle down her cheek. "You probably blocked this out of your head or something. I don't think you would be sitting next to me right now if you remembered. But you need to know this Mel." Mel's mom took another deep breath and said, "Honey, I used to beat the crap out of you. The day I dropped you off, you had a busted lip, your eyes were swollen… almost swollen shut… your… your arm was broken too."

"Your uncle wanted to call the cops on me, but Jane stopped him. She told me to leave you with her and not to come back until I could take care of myself and you. I just never got to the point where I could take care of me. I got deeper into drugs and I was hooking for a while. I finally got arrested for robbing a liquor store."

Mel shook her head from confusion; her eyes brimmed with more tears. "What? That isn't true. You never abused me. You would never do the things you just said. Tell me the truth!"

"I am Mel," her mom let go of her hands and crossed her arms. Mel suddenly felt cold and started to shiver. "I'm sorry Mel. I do want you to know that I thought about you every day. Believe it or not, I truly only wanted the best for you."

Sudden images of a belt flashed across Mel's mind. Images of herself as a little girl curled up in the corner of a room crying begging, "Please no more. I'm sorry mama." Mel flinched and looked at her mother again. She remembered something vividly. "If that were true why would you slap me in the face with a belt buckle?" Mel had a horrified expression on her face. "For the longest time I thought the memories were just bad dreams but the reality was they were appalling memories." Mel felt the taste of bile rise up to her mouth.

Mel stood up and paced around the hotel room. She stopped for a moment to take her shoes off then she resumed back to pacing. Her mom remained on the bed with her arms crossed. "Mel, I'm not the same person I was when I left. I went through extensive rehab and I've been clean for ten years. I just got married last year. I work at a department store in Phoenix, Arizona right now."

"Okay, so now what?" Mel asked. She stood in front of the television with her arms crossed. "You've met me again. So now what do we do?"

"We hang out together while I'm here visiting. We get to know each other again. We call each other, email, IM, text... whatever. We just stay in contact."

"I don't know if I can do that," Mel said. Her heart felt cold.

"But…" her mom stuttered from flustered frustration, "Mel…. Reggie flew me out here…"

"He can fly you back."

"Mel, I am not going to go anywhere until you give me another hug and we set a time and date for us to meet again."

"Don't try to force me to love you."

"I'm not attempting to force you into loving me, Mel. I know it's hard for you to look at me right now and I know I made many mistakes. I treated you wrong. The one thing I am sure I did right, though… was giving birth to you. The second right thing I did was leaving you with my brother and Jane. You've turned out to be a beautiful and loving person. I hope that never changes."

Mel wasn't sure how she should feel. She wasn't sure if she should embrace the woman who was sitting on the bed across from her or throw her out because of the past and present pain she had caused.

Mel licked her lips and said, "Mom, I am glad that you let me know who you were and who you are now. But I can't just open my arms out to you and allow you to be a constant in my life right now."

"I understand but just schedule me in for another meeting, please. I need you in my life, Mel, even if it is only once in a long while."

Mel put her head down for a long minute. She stared down at her bare feet. Finally she said, "Okay, why don't we exchange phone numbers and start speaking to each other on the phone first, all right?"

"Okay," her mom said as she stood up. She hugged Mel one more time then said, "Well, I guess I will go now. You look exhausted."

"I am," Mel said as she opened the hotel room door. Her mom took it as her queue and walked out of the hotel room.

Mel was alone for half an hour before Reggie reappeared. She explained to him what happened. Reggie was shocked.

"I remember now Aunt Jane taking me to the emergency room," Mel explained, recalling the day she was abandoned. "We were there all night. They put a cast on me and gave me a bunch of painkillers. I had my arm in a cast for six weeks. I also remember my Aunt Jane wrapped a beautiful scarf around my cast." Mel tilted her head to the side trying to recall something else, "The scarf was navy blue with little butterflies on it."

Reggie held Mel in a quiet hug for a few minutes. Finally, she pulled away and looked up at him, "Reggie, why would you do something like that? What were you thinking?"

"Remember when we were in Hawaii and you were upset that your mother wasn't at the wedding?"

"Yes."

"Well, I told you before I don't ever want to see you upset."

"Oh, because my lips get big and puffy and my eyes swell up as if I were hit with a mighty fist."

Reggie moved closer to her and held her tightly. "Yes, that has something to do with it but mostly because when you hurt, I hurt too. When I saw you feeling sad and empty inside, I felt helpless... like I was useless and I wasn't fulfilling my duty as your husband. So I asked Pablo if he knew someone who could help find your mom. He put me in contact with a private investigator named Cedrick... Terrence thought it was a great idea."

"Reggie, there will be plenty of times when I will feel down and empty inside. You can't rescue me all the time."

"Mel, I know that I can't save you all the time and I know that you have to figure out a lot about yourself. Like whether or not you are going to call your mom back."

"Would you think I am an awful person if I didn't call her back?"

"No, you have every right to feel that way."

"Really?" Mel asked. She felt a little-relieved hearing Reggie say that.

"Yes," Reggie answered then continued while holding her hands, "It's like what Terrence had said about Lisa one time. They will stay together when the already rough surface starts to crumble. They will pick up the pieces, use some super glue or a superb glue gun and piece it all together. Then we can put some fresh paint on it and make it look like new. You may be able to see some of the cracks, but it kind of adds more character and appeal to it... kind of like.... You know what you're getting... you know?"

"What?" Mel asked utterly confused.

He said quietly, "It means I'm here for you always."

She smiled and kissed him. She knew with certainty her friends would always be there too.

Epilogue

Three years later…

Veronica and Melody were laughing as they were jumping up and down in the bouncing house. Pablo peeked his head inside and said, "Um… ladies… don't you think it's time to let your kids have their turn?" Veronica and Melody both stopped jumping and pouted.

"Fine… party pooper…" Veronica squeezed through the opening and slipped her sandals back on. Mel soon followed. Reggie was standing close by holding their one-year-old son, Ray. Mel held her hands out and Ray reached out for her, squeezing his little arms tightly around her neck and planting a wet slobbery kiss on her lips. Mel grinned.

"Can your brother go in now too?" Mel's mom asked, holding a two-year-old who looked so much like Mel.

"I guess since it is his birthday we're celebrating… we should allow him to go now, don't you think?"

Veronica laughed. "Yes, but I think we have to go in and make sure they don't get carried away." She winked.

Melody glanced around Pablo and Veronica's backyard. It was full of family and friends who came to celebrate her little brother's birthday. She smiled at her mom and Reggie. There had been rough and tough moments, but eventually everything came together. Her mom and step-dad decided to move close by. She finally felt full from the love of family and great friends.